OMINOUS CHOICES

To Joe, Katy, and Peter Carlson

TABLE OF CONTENTS

THE YOUNG TRIBULATION FORCE

Original members—Vicki Byrne, Judd
Thompson, Lionel Washington

Other members—Mark, Conrad, Darrion,
Janie, Charlie, Shelly, Melinda

OTHER BELIEVERS

Chang Wong—Chinese teenager working in
New Babylon

Tsion Ben-Judah—Jewish scholar who writes
about prophecy

Colin and Becky Dial—Wisconsin couple

Sam Goldberg—Jewish teenager, Lionel's
good friend

Mr. Mitchell Stein—Jewish friend of the
Young Trib Force

Naomi Tiberius—computer whiz living
in Petra

Chaim Rosenzweig—famous Israeli scientist

Tanya Spivey—daughter of Mountain Militia
leader, Cyrus Spivey

Cheryl Tifanne—pregnant young lady from Iowa

Zeke Zuckermandel—disguise specialist for the Tribulation Force

Marshall Jameson—leader of the Avery, Wisconsin believers

UNBELIEVERS

Nicolae Carpathia—leader of the Global Community

Leon Fortunato—Carpathia's right-hand man

What's Gone On Before

JUDD Thompson Jr. and the rest of the Young Tribulation Force are living the adventure of a lifetime. Judd and Lionel Washington escape bounty hunters in South Carolina and rush inland.

Vicki Byrne and the others at the western Wisconsin hideout repair cabins and reach out to people through the Internet. Vicki desperately wants to help Judd and Lionel, but they're too far away. In addition to bounty hunters, the kids must elude citizens who are rewarded for killing anyone without Carpathia's mark.

Sam Goldberg and Mitchell Stein fly from Petra to Tel Aviv to speak with the sons of Rabbi Ben-Eliezar. Sam and Mr. Stein are thrown into prison with Aron Ben-Eliezar, and God miraculously releases them.

Since travel is so dangerous with the vigilante law in effect, Judd and Lionel travel north on foot, visiting a series of safe houses as they slowly make their way back to their friends in Wisconsin.

Vicki is excited to hear about Judd's progress and speaks with him frequently by phone. In the back of her mind are the words of an angel who warned that someone she loved would not return "whole." Cheryl Tifanne becomes ill, and Vicki fears the girl is going to have her baby early. While others go for help, Vicki tries to calm Cheryl.

After a long stay in Indiana, Judd and Lionel set out for the final leg of their trek. Just before midnight, Lionel climbs down a steep embankment while Judd waits above on a huge boulder. Suddenly the rock tips and Judd jumps, the rock plunging after him.

Join the Young Tribulation Force as they face some of the most desperate days of their lives and struggle to survive the Great Tribulation.

ONE

Pinned

JUDD Thompson Jr. let go of the bush and scampered to his left, trying to escape certain death. Tiny rocks fell as he searched for footing, his feet pumping like a cartoon character's. Lionel was down there, but all Judd could think about was getting out of the way.

Judd lunged for a flat rock and hung on with both hands. He glanced back as the rock reared in the air like a stony stallion and hovered, blocking the clouds and sky. Just as he thought he would be squashed, the rock tipped to the right and began a free fall toward the bottom. Smaller rocks and dust covered Judd's face.

The ground shuddered with each turn of the rock. Judd pulled himself to a sitting position while the boulder crashed to the bottom.

As the dust settled and Judd caught his breath, he looked for Lionel. He had had plenty of time to get out of the way, and Judd wondered if he had jumped into the bushes by the stream.

"Guess we should have gone around, huh?" Judd called out.

No response.

"That rock was as big as a house. Good thing we got out of the way."

Still no response.

"Hey, Lionel, where are you?"

Crickets chirped and frogs croaked. Hearing the trickle of water gave Judd an eerie feeling. Everything was peaceful, as if nothing had happened.

"Come on, man, this isn't funny. You think I tried to knock that rock down?"

Judd surveyed the damage. The crashing rock had left several craters in its wake, which would make it even more difficult to get down. Any moment he expected Lionel to jump out from behind a bush and scold him.

Judd carefully took a few steps left to a small ridge. As he slowly climbed down, something hissed near his foot. He jumped and slid a few feet. When he heard the hiss again, he leaped to the ground, a good fifteen-foot drop.

His knees ached after the fall, but he was glad to be away from the snake. "Lionel?"

Judd listened closely. Rocks skittered down the hill and came to rest near him. Either Lionel was hiding in the bushes or . . .

"Lionel, I just heard a snake."

Something moved and moaned softly. Judd called Lionel's name again, but only crickets and frogs responded. Something swooped over him, a fluttering of wings and a caw. Judd ducked, then saw the outline of a crow against the night sky. When the bird lighted in a nearby tree, Judd moved toward the boulder. What he saw when he rounded the corner took his breath away.

※

Vicki Byrne held Cheryl Tifanne's hand and prayed with all her might. Vicki feared the baby was in trouble, but the greater fear was that Cheryl was about to deliver it without the help of the midwife.

Sweat poured from Cheryl's forehead, the girl turning her head from side to side and moaning. When the cabin door opened and Vicki turned, Cheryl dug her fingernails into Vicki's arm.

"Don't leave me," Cheryl said through clenched teeth.

"Don't worry."

Shelly came in with Josey Fogarty. Josey carried a box and placed it on the nightstand. "There's some pain medication in here—"

"Good," Vicki said, grabbing a bottle.

"Wait," Josey said. "If she's in labor, she shouldn't take anything."

"I need something for the pain!" Cheryl screamed.

Josey pulled Vicki's arm and whispered, "This medicine will go right to the baby. It could endanger the child."

"But don't they give women medicine for pain before they have their babies?" Vicki said. "That's what happened with my mom."

"They can give them all kinds of things, but the patients are on monitors, checking heartbeats and oxygen levels. We don't have any equipment, and the medicine is the wrong kind."

"Vicki!" Cheryl shouted.

"I'm right here," Vicki said, then turned back to Josey. "We have to give her something."

"Not until we know for sure what's happening," Josey said.

Shelly reached in her pocket, and plastic rattled. She pulled out a half-eaten roll of candy. "We could give her this."

"That won't do anything," Vicki said.

4

"But if she thinks it's medicine, maybe it'll calm her down."

Josey nodded. "It's worth a try."

"Give me one," Vicki said.

Cheryl's hands shook as she sat up and grabbed a glass of water. She popped the piece of candy in her mouth without looking at it and downed the glass, water dripping from the corners of her mouth and onto her bedsheets. Cheryl closed her eyes and lay back, trying to catch her breath.

"Try to relax," Josey said. "You and the baby are going to be fine."

"Is the doctor coming?" Cheryl said.

"She's a midwife—it's like a doctor, without the hospital," Vicki said.

"How long before she comes?" Cheryl gasped.

"Won't be long," Vicki said as she glanced at Shelly and Josey.

Vicki had been in the room during part of her mother's labor with her little sister, Jeanni. It had been a long process, and Vicki hadn't seen the worst of it, certainly not the kind of pain Cheryl was going through.

"Call Marshall and ask him if there's anything else we can do for her," Vicki whispered to Shelly. "The minute he makes contact with that midwife, have him call us."

Vicki took Cheryl's temperature and it was normal. "Stay still. Help will be here soon."

⁕

Judd moved around the rock, horrified. Lionel lay motionless on the ground. The left side of his body appeared to be pinned under the boulder.

Judd stared at the scene, unable to move. Was Lionel breathing? Had the rock crushed the life from him? Judd finally knelt and placed a hand on Lionel's neck. *A pulse.*

Lionel's head lolled to the side, and he opened his eyes. "It hurts."

"What does?"

"My arm."

Judd let his eyes adjust to the dim light. He had thought Lionel's whole body was under the rock, but only his left arm was pinned. "I'll have you out of here in a few minutes, just hang on."

"I'm not going anywhere," Lionel mumbled.

Judd looked around for something to wedge under the rock and came back with the biggest stick he could find. He shoved it as far under the rock as he could and pushed, but the wood cracked. He had a sinking feeling there was no way the rock would move.

"Hold on. I'm going to try something else," Judd said.

Lionel said something and Judd leaned close. "What?"

"Backpack . . . can you get it off?"

Judd pulled one side of Lionel's backpack off, then loosened the strap on the other side and pulled it free. He placed it under Lionel's head, and the boy sighed and nodded.

Judd found a sharp rock near the stream and began digging a few feet from Lionel's trapped arm. He hoped to dig a hole big enough to pull Lionel free, but a few scrapes against the earth and his heart sank. Lionel was pinned under a rock weighing thousands of pounds. Without some kind of jack or mechanical device, he was stuck.

Judd ran a hand through his hair and took the cell phone from his backpack. He dialed the safe house in Salem, but there was no answer. There was no one to call, no one he could think of to help. He would enlist the prayer support of others in the Young Tribulation Force, of course, but where else could he turn? He and Lionel were on their own.

Judd walked toward the stream again, racking his brain. If only they had gone around the hill. If only he hadn't sat on the boulder.

"God, you sent that angel, Anak, to Vicki

and the others. It would only take one finger for him to lift this rock and help Lionel. Please, I need your help. I need to get Lionel out of there, and there's simply no way."

Judd walked back to his friend and sat. "How're you feeling?"

Lionel's eyes fluttered. "I tried to get out of the way, but I tripped. I'm lucky the rock didn't roll one more time or I'd be flat as a manhole cover." He took a breath and blew it out. "There's no way to get me out, is there?"

"There's a way. I just haven't found it yet." Judd rummaged through his backpack and pulled out a flashlight. Though the area surrounding him was bathed in moonlight, under the rock it was dark. Judd switched the flashlight on and pointed it toward Lionel's trapped arm. Blood streaked Lionel's shirt and pooled in the dirt.

If I don't get him out of here, he could bleed to death.

Vicki looked for any improvement in Cheryl's condition but found none. The girl thrashed and squirmed, holding her stomach. When the phone rang, Vicki thought it was Marshall with the midwife. She quickly answered but heard Judd's voice.

"We've got a situation here," Judd said with emotion. "There's been an accident."

"What happened? Are you all right?"

"I'm fine. A little scratched up, but fine." After he explained what had happened to Lionel, Vicki covered the phone and relayed the message to the others.

"Tell everybody to pray," Judd said. "I need wisdom about what to do."

"He should put a tourniquet on that arm to stop the bleeding," Josey said, taking the phone. "You have to make this decision carefully, Judd, but if you think there's no chance to save that arm—"

Judd interrupted and Vicki strained to hear but couldn't. Finally, Josey said, "If the bleeding doesn't stop, you have to stop it. A tourniquet will do that. At least he won't bleed to death."

The two talked a few minutes, and Josey handed the phone back to Vicki. "Judd, can you get back to the last safe house and get help?"

"It's an option, but not a very good one."

Vicki explained what was going on with Cheryl, and Judd said he would pray for her. Judd promised he would call and give them an update by morning.

When she hung up, Vicki felt low. Cheryl's

condition seemed worse, and Lionel was in grave danger. She asked Conrad to carefully word a prayer alert and send it over the kids' Web site.

Shelly put a hand on Vicki's shoulder. "God's going to help us. I'm sure of it."

Vicki nodded. "I just wish he would hurry."

Judd pointed the flashlight under the rock. The boulder completely covered Lionel's hand and forearm, but there was a small crevice that left Lionel's elbow uncovered. His arm was swollen, and blood pulsed from the wound.

"How do you feel?" Judd said.

Lionel blinked. "My head feels kind of light, like I'm going to be sick."

Judd examined the arm and concluded that Lionel's hand and forearm were crushed. Whether they would ever heal once he got out of there—if he got out of there—Judd didn't know. But from what Josey said, his first priority was to stop the bleeding.

"I'm going to put a tourniquet around your arm before I leave," Judd said.

"Leave? Where are you going?"

"For help. There's no way I can move this

thing. Maybe I can get back to the people in Salem."

"Even if they come, how are they going to move it?"

"That place was an old farm equipment store. They're bound to have something. A couple of inches and you're out of there."

"Then what?" Lionel said.

Judd patted Lionel's shoulder. "We'll figure that out." He took off his belt and carefully strapped it around Lionel's arm above the elbow. He pulled it tight, and Lionel winced as Judd made a mark on the belt for the new hole. "Where's your knife?"

"Left front pants pocket. Sorry, but I can't reach it at the moment."

Judd smiled. That Lionel still had a sense of humor was a good sign. Judd found the knife and spent several minutes jabbing a hole in the belt. "This isn't going to feel good, but it's necessary."

"Whatever," Lionel said.

Judd took a breath, then pulled the belt as tight as he could around Lionel's arm. Lionel's scream echoed through the woods, and Judd nearly let go, but he knew this was Lionel's best chance of getting out alive.

Lionel wiped his forehead with his right hand. "Sorry I yelled like that."

"Don't be," Judd said, putting the knife in Lionel's right pocket. He pulled out the cell phone and dialed the safe house in Salem again. No answer. Judd handed the phone to Lionel. "Keep this and call Vicki if you need someone to talk to."

"But you might need it."

Judd shook his head and opened Lionel's backpack. He sorted the food and made sure Lionel could get to it, then gave Lionel all but one bottle of water. "I'll be back before sunup. Sundown tonight at the latest. Can you hang in there that long?"

"Only one way to find out," Lionel said. "Don't take any chances back there."

Judd nodded and checked Lionel's arm to make sure the bleeding had stopped.

"There'll be a lot of people praying for you. Concentrate on staying alive."

"That's been my full-time job since the disappearances."

Judd grabbed his flashlight from the backpack, headed into the night, and took a final look back. Lionel waved and tried to smile.

TWO

Chang's Bad News

VICKI held Cheryl's hand and looked out the window. How could they have been so wrong about the due date? Was the baby in danger? Maybe it had already died.

Vicki shook her head. She couldn't think that way. They had to assume it was alive and work as hard as they could.

Cheryl squeezed Vicki's arm. Her breathing was short and her hands shook. "Something's wrong, isn't it?" Cheryl panted. "Am I going to lose the baby?"

Vicki patted her shoulder. "This just took us by surprise. You're a little early, but Marshall will get help. As soon as he gets back we'll all feel a lot better."

Cheryl put her head on the pillow and grimaced. Her breathing came rapidly, along with short moans of pain.

"Where does it hurt?" Vicki said.

Cheryl grabbed low on her stomach. "There's a lot of pressure. It feels like my stomach's going to explode."

The girl leaned forward, and Vicki noticed wetness on Cheryl's pants. Cheryl gasped.

Josey rushed to them. "Don't be scared. That was just your water breaking."

"What water?"

"A sac of fluid protects the baby. If it breaks, it usually means the baby is moving further down. We're going to see that little one tonight."

When Josey moved in to help Cheryl, Vicki stepped out of the way. Vicki wasn't ready for this. The baby couldn't be born tonight, could it? In the last few months Vicki had read lots on the Internet about giving birth. She had walked Cheryl through a class on how to breathe during labor, but now, all her reading and coaching seemed worthless. She felt helpless, without a clue about what would happen next.

She whispered the only prayer she could think of. "God, help us."

⁕

Judd went as fast as he could toward the stream, pointing his flashlight at the bank

14

and making sure of his footing. It would take extra time going around the hill this way, but he wouldn't risk climbing up and sending more rocks onto Lionel.

Judd talked as he walked, trying to keep himself moving. His words became prayers as he asked God for wisdom. He prayed for Cheryl, the baby, and that Vicki would be able to help. He asked God to bring Marshall and the midwife back quickly and to spare the life of this child.

But Judd's thoughts kept coming back to Lionel. Had he checked the bleeding well enough? If the tourniquet wasn't tight, Lionel could die. Judd cringed as he imagined getting back to the rock and finding Lionel's body.

Judd stepped onto a rock jutting out over the stream. "God, I've got to trust you to take care of Lionel. You have to show yourself mighty in this, because I'm too weak to do anything else."

Judd moved through the darkened woods as quickly as he could. Someone at the safe house had to help.

Lionel wanted to scream for Judd to turn around. He didn't want to be left alone, but he knew it was his only chance. Every breath sent pain pulsing and throbbing through his arm.

Lying on his back in the rocks and dirt was the most uncomfortable position he could think of. *This is where I'll spend the next few hours, so I'd better get used to it.*

Lionel mustered the strength to pull the backpack closer with his right hand. Judd had emptied the contents on the ground so it would be easier to grab the cell phone, his flashlight, or something to eat. He bunched the backpack up and put his head back, out of breath. Pain shot through his arm and shoulder.

Lionel felt something move on his neck, and he smacked it. Whether it was a spider or some other insect he didn't know. The warmth of his skin probably attracted it, he thought. *And if I attract spiders, what else will I find out here?*

The stream caught his attention, and he tried to concentrate on it instead of the pain. His mom had bought a noise reducer for his room when he was young, so growing up he had gone to sleep to electronic crickets, a heartbeat, or a babbling brook. The only problem with the water sound was that it made his younger brother, Ronnie, want to go to the bathroom. His mom would kiss them good night, turn on the device, and leave. As soon as she was out the door, so was Ronnie, hopping sideways to the bathroom.

The thought made Lionel laugh, which also made his arm hurt. He listened to the water running over the smooth rocks and tried to imagine what it looked like in the moonlight. Such a peaceful sound. He could go to sleep so easily listening to that.

No! He couldn't go to sleep. If he went to sleep, he might never wake up. He put a finger on his arm just below the belt Judd had tightened. There was blood, he was sure of it. No way was he going to sleep.

Lionel grabbed a peanut-butter sandwich with his free hand and unwrapped it. Supplies at the Salem safe house had dwindled, but the people had given them enough food for two days. Lionel didn't know how long it had been since he had eaten a cheeseburger or any meat. Without the mark of the beast, those hiding had to settle for any food they could scrounge up or what the Commodity Co-op could provide. That usually meant something out of a can and stale bread. Lionel pretended the sandwich was a juicy burger from his favorite restaurant.

How long had it been since he had eaten at a restaurant, walked through a mall, shopped for clothes, or listened to music on the radio? How long since he had done anything *normal*? The disappearances of his family had been a little more than four years ago, but it seemed like a lifetime.

Four years. Lionel was now seventeen. He should have been looking for his first car, stashing cash to buy some old beater he could call his own.

He winced as another wave of pain hit. Lionel thought of his father. Charles had been a heavy-equipment operator. If he were here, he'd have this rock off in no time. But he wasn't, and Lionel wouldn't see him again until . . .

Lionel reached for his sandwich but dropped it. He started to blow away the dust and tiny rocks stuck to the jelly, but he wasn't hungry anymore. He put the sandwich back on the wrapper and pushed it aside.

Lionel closed his eyes and imagined his father sitting in a crane, lifting the huge rock. His dad could always fix things, and Lionel couldn't remember him ever failing at mechanical work. The only thing that threw him was dealing with Lionel's older sister, Clarice. She knew how to push his buttons and get him flustered. A two-ton rock would have been a piece of cake, but an argument with Clarice, that was something else.

The pain returned, and Lionel reached for a bottle of water. Judd had forgotten to loosen the top, so Lionel struggled to unscrew it. He tried holding it under his arm, but the bottle slipped. Finally, he put the cap in his mouth and cracked the seal, sending a dribble of water down his neck. Lionel took a drink and screwed the cap back on.

Something moved in the bushes by the stream, and Lionel instinctively tried to sit up, sending a new wave of pain through his left arm. He cried out, then lay back and turned toward the bushes. "Judd?"

No answer.

"Hey, no fair trying to scare me!"

Crickets and frogs and the stream. *Is it my imagination?* He found the flashlight and flicked it on. Just before the flurry and scurry of feet, Lionel saw two eyes.

Vicki tried to calm Cheryl as she prepared to deliver the baby. Shelly helped Cheryl get into a clean nightshirt while Josey put new sheets on the bed. Tom Fogarty, the former cop, offered to help. Josey thanked him, and Vicki noticed Charlie pacing outside the door of the cabin.

When Cheryl was settled, Conrad pulled

Vicki outside and showed her a printout of responses to the prayer alert. "We've had more than a hundred notes so far, and it's only been on the Web site a few minutes."

"We're going to need the support," Vicki said.

"How close is she?"

"Josey thinks it could be soon. I hope Marshall hurries."

"Mark's with him. He'll call as soon as they find the midwife."

When Cheryl screamed again, Vicki rushed to the door. Charlie grabbed her arm. "If there's anything I can do, let me know."

Vicki nodded and ran into the cabin.

※

Lionel couldn't breathe for a few seconds as the animal disappeared into the bushes. He couldn't tell what or how large it was. *Great,* he thought, *now I'm being stalked.*

Lionel picked up the ant-covered sandwich. *Did the food attract the animal? Maybe it was my blood.*

Throughout their trip from South Carolina, Judd and Lionel had seen animals. Moving mostly at night, the two had run across opossums and skunks, but they had also seen several coyotes and what looked like wolves.

Lionel waved the flashlight, trying to catch the eyes again. A shrill sound split the night. *The cell phone!* Lionel reached for it but knocked it away. He strained, popping something in his left arm. He screamed in pain, then grabbed the phone. When he caught his breath, he pushed the receive button. "Hello?"

"Judd? It's Chang."

Lionel told Chang where Judd was and what had happened.

"I'm surprised you're still able to talk," Chang said. "Have you taken anything for the pain?"

"We didn't bring any medicine."

Chang asked for his location and punched in the coordinates on his computer. "I have to be careful about how much I try to do these days. They're still after that pesky mole in the palace." He clicked the keyboard and sighed. "The closest group of believers is where you've just come from. But . . ."

"What is it?"

A few more clicks. "Oh no."

"Tell me what you see."

"Do you have any way to get in touch with Judd?"

"No. I have the phone with me."

"The Global Community is conducting a midnight raid on that group. Judd could be walking into a trap."

Lionel's heart beat wildly. "We have to pray he sees them before he gets there."

Chang prayed and said he would check in later. The phone call had sapped Lionel's strength, and he wondered what had popped in his arm. He reached for the belt Judd had tightened and felt blood, but it seemed thicker. He put his head on the backpack, closed his eyes, and thought about the people in Salem. He and Judd had stayed with them longer than anyone else on their trip north, and though tempers had flared at times because of the close quarters, Lionel had a deep respect and love for the people.

Lionel imagined the GC storming the place, finding the hideout, and hauling the people out one by one. The GC loved torching things during their raids to destroy evidence and instill fear in believers. With the vigilante law in effect, his friends would be unable to escape.

A sickening thought raced through Lionel's mind. Had he and Judd been the reason the group was discovered? Had someone seen them stealing away earlier and called the Global Community? The idea turned Lionel's stomach.

Something moved to Lionel's right, and he grabbed the flashlight. A flash of red. Two eyes darted through the bushes and were gone.

Then something hissed to his right. Judd had said something about a snake when he was coming down the hill. Maybe it was his mind playing tricks. Maybe the whole thing—

Hiss . . .

Lionel slowly turned his head and came face-to-face with a coiled snake, only a few inches from his face.

THREE

Visitors

LIONEL froze in horror. He had never liked snakes. When he was a kid, he couldn't bring himself to touch a page with a snake's picture on it. He'd had nightmares of hundreds of snakes writhing in his front yard. Those dreams sent him to his mom and dad's room quicker than the noise reducer sent Ronnie to the bathroom.

Lionel was close enough to see the snake's tongue slither in and out of its mouth. He looked at its eyes and thought of the nature show he had seen that said you could tell if a snake was poisonous by the shape of its head. The snake didn't rattle, but the markings were strange. Perhaps it was a copperhead.

The thing is probably looking for food, Lionel told himself. *He'll realize I'm too big and go away.*

The snake inched closer, angling toward the rock and Lionel's trapped arm.

"Nice snake," Lionel whispered, then rolled his eyes. *I'm talking to the thing like it's a puppy.*

The snake's head pulled back a few inches, and Lionel was sure it would strike. He closed his eyes and fumbled for the flashlight or phone, anything to throw.

Movement in the bush startled him, and a small animal jumped out and danced around the snake, pawing and nipping. *A fox!* The snake retreated, trying to find safety under the huge rock, but the fox hopped forward, blocking its way and dodging the snake's strikes.

Lionel wanted to cheer the fox on, but he was afraid it would scare the animal. Instead, he lay still and watched the action, silently praying.

The fox chased its enemy to the hillside and out of sight, but Lionel wondered if the snake was really gone. He had always heard that snakes don't attack people unless you enter their territory, but he'd never believed it.

He closed his eyes and took a breath. Though he hadn't moved, the excitement of the encounter had raised his heart rate. His skin glistened with sweat, and the cool air of the early morning gave him a chill.

The fox returned, sniffing at the air by the

rock and licking its paws. The animal was thin and wiry, and Lionel could see its hipbones sticking out. The fox didn't pay attention to Lionel, as if this heroic act were a normal part of its day.

"Hey, boy, thanks for the help," Lionel whispered.

The fox looked up. Lionel expected it to bolt, but it just stared at him. Lionel picked up the sandwich, and the fox darted backward toward the hill, then slowly sniffed at the air.

"I have something for you, if you want it. It's not much, but it's all I have. You want it?" Lionel held out the sandwich, hoping the fox would approach.

Instead, it sat, studying the food and the teenager. It put its front paws on the ground and stretched.

Suddenly, Lionel felt a wave of pain and nausea. Whether it was the adrenaline rush of the encounter with the snake or too much blood loss he couldn't tell, but he felt tired and cold. He draped the backpack over him just before he lost consciousness.

Vicki talked with Marshall by phone, the man giving instructions for what they should do. Mark was driving to the midwife's house, and they were still a few miles away. "Make Cheryl as comfortable as possible," Marshall said. "We'll call as soon as we find her."

"Her water broke, and she's feeling a lot of pressure," Vicki said.

Marshall paused. "So she's further along than we thought. Okay, Wanda doesn't use a phone, but she might be by her computer. Write her."

Vicki found the address for the midwife and quickly wrote a message, asking if there was anything more they could do for Cheryl. As she waited, Vicki noticed reports about miracle workers from around the world. These were the new breed of Nicolae's messiahs, changing water to wine, healing the sick, and doing various magic tricks to confuse the world.

A return message from Wanda came a few minutes later.

> *Your friend is going to want to push, but don't let her. The passage the baby has to come through has to dilate—or open up enough for the baby's head to come through. There's a chance she could be ready, but from what you've said I doubt it. I can tell you how to check, but I'd rather be there. Get a watch and figure out how*

*many minutes between contractions. Your
friends in the car should be close to me. If
they have a phone, I'll call you from the
road.*

Wanda

Vicki borrowed Conrad's watch and
hurried back to Cheryl. When a contraction
came, her stomach tightened, she closed her
eyes, and grabbed whatever was near. The
first contraction lasted about forty-five
seconds. Vicki pressed the stopwatch button
and counted.

One minute.

Josey put another pillow behind Cheryl
and encouraged her to relax until the next
contraction.

Two minutes.

Vicki watched the timer count up, praying
more time would pass before the pain began
again.

Three minutes.

Shelly took Vicki's arm in hers. "Are you
ready to become Aunt Vicki?"

Vicki forced a smile. "Aunt Vicki is fine.
I'm just not ready for Dr. Vicki."

"Ow, ow, ow!" Cheryl screamed. "Here it
comes again!"

Vicki glanced at the watch. Three minutes, twenty-eight seconds.

※

Lionel opened his eyes slowly. It was still dark, but he had no idea how long he had been asleep. Five minutes? An hour? A slight wind blew from the east and he shivered.

The fox was close, sniffing at the sandwich in Lionel's hand. Lionel remained still and watched the animal inch forward like a hungry pup. It licked at the peanut butter and backed away, then moved forward again and took a bite. When it came back for more, Lionel let go, and the fox pulled the sandwich near the rock and devoured it.

"Hope you enjoy that," Lionel whispered. "You deserve it."

Lionel felt strangely comforted by the animal and wondered if God had sent it. Could an angel appear as a fox? He shook his head. The loss of blood was even affecting his theology.

Lionel tried to think of a verse that applied to his situation. There was something in the Psalms about God being a refuge in times of trouble. In other places it described God as a rock, but Lionel didn't want to think about that. He reached for his left arm again and noticed the blood was almost dry. The tourniquet had worked.

He sipped some water and watched the fox lick its lips. The sandwich was gone, and there was nothing to keep the animal near. Still, it stayed, and Lionel was grateful.

※

As soon as Judd had gotten past the hill and the stream, he quickened his pace and ran toward Salem over the path they had followed. Normally, he and Lionel watched the compass and headed northwest, making sure they stayed in the woods or other places with few people. The jog back seemed unfamiliar, but Judd knew he was going in the right direction. When he finally reached the edge of town, he got his bearings and headed for the hideout.

Judd prayed for Lionel as he ran. What had begun as the last leg of their journey had turned into a nightmare. In the past few months two of his friends had died at the hands of the Global Community. Chang Wong, his contact in New Babylon, constantly lived under the pressure of being watched inside Nicolae Carpathia's palace. The farther Judd ran, the angrier he became at Carpathia, GC Peacekeepers, Morale Monitors, bounty hunters, and Satan himself.

Judd stopped by a tree a hundred yards from the hideout and caught his breath. He realized he was angry, not just at the evil around him but also at God for allowing it. The whole thing was somehow part of God's plan, but Judd didn't understand it.

A sudden flash in the distance caught his attention. Judd studied the landscape in the moonlight and figured it was the reflection of headlights on a window. He moved into the open pasture, angling toward a barn and running close to the ground.

A single beam of light swept over the field. Judd hit the ground immediately and rolled, trying to find a low point. The beam swept over him just as he spun into a dip in the field.

Judd wondered who would be out at this time of night. He waited a few minutes, listening for voices, but only heard cars in the distance. When enough time had gone by, he peeked toward the light but saw nothing. He rose and darted toward the barn. Suddenly, a radio crackled and Judd's heart sank. He reached the barn and put his back flat against the outside wall. He was in shadows and felt safer, but he had to get a look at the safe house.

He crept through shadows inside the barn. Though it still smelled of hay and animals, it was empty, save for an old hay baler and some rusted plows. He climbed into the loft, the soft moonlight shining through the weathered boards.

Judd pressed his face close to a hole and spotted the farm machine shop where he and Lionel had stayed. Several men stood at the side of the building. An orange glow appeared, and Judd realized a few people were smoking.

No one at the hideout smokes, Judd thought, *and they wouldn't be outside anyway.*

Judd had a bad feeling the safe house wasn't so safe. He looked out another opening in the barn and spied an old tractor parked a few yards away. Judd wanted to find help for Lionel, but he had to make sure his friends at the safe house were okay.

Within a few minutes after finishing the sandwich, the fox left. Lionel felt more alone than ever. He nearly cried when the little red animal turned and headed into the woods.

"Okay, Lord," Lionel prayed aloud, "you were good enough to send me someone to keep me company and chase that snake away. Now I need somebody strong enough to lift this rock."

The crickets and frogs lulled Lionel back to sleep.

＊

Judd crawled the final few yards to the abandoned tractor and hid behind its massive wheel. He counted five men by the door to the safe house. They kept quiet, looking out at the field.

Finally, a man in a GC uniform approached, and the men stood at attention. "Commander Fulcire wants you to know you'll be rewarded for your actions tonight," the Peacekeeper said. "Because of your alertness, we were able to detain a number of unmarked citizens tonight."

The group applauded, then whooped again when they heard they would divide the bounty for each of the citizens equally.

"Though the prisoners wouldn't give information before they were . . . uh, taken care of," the Peacekeeper said, "we believe the first report to be true. There are two more heading north, and if you'd like to be part of that search party, follow me."

After the group went inside the former safe house, Judd caught his breath. Someone had seen Lionel and him leaving the safe house. Judd had to throw these men off the track and get help to Lionel before they found him. But how?

Judd duckwalked to the GC cruiser, reached through the open window, and grabbed the microphone to the radio. "All GC Peacekeepers, repeat, all GC Peace- keepers," Judd said in an official tone, "we have an alert of two unmarked citizens now crossing Highway 56, just east of town. These may be the two spotted earlier. Out."

Judd threw the microphone into the car and hustled back to his hiding place. The men poured from the building followed by the Peacekeeper who tugged at the micro- phone on his shoulder.

"Verify that last transmission," the Peace- keeper said.

The radio remained silent, but already the men had jumped in their cars and were racing toward the highway. Judd didn't know how long he had before they figured out his call was a hoax, but he knew he had to look for help somewhere else. He glanced at the sky. Only a few more hours before daylight.

Vicki counted the minutes between contractions. A few came within two minutes of each other, while others came five minutes or more apart. Cheryl grew weaker with each round of contractions, sometimes writhing and shouting in pain. Josey did what she could to keep the girl calm but gave Vicki a worried look. Cheryl was panting, taking in short gasps of air between screams. Josey whispered that Cheryl could pass out from lack of oxygen if she didn't breathe slower.

On the next contraction, Cheryl let out a piercing scream. "I can't take it anymore! I want to push. I have to!"

"Call Marshall," Josey said, holding Cheryl down.

Shelly stood at the foot of the bed. "Guys, look at this!"

Vicki rushed to Shelly's side and gasped. She could see the top of the baby's head in the birth canal.

FOUR

Ryan Victor

VICKI felt a mix of awe and fear. Her mouth dropped open at the sight of the baby's head, but she nearly fainted when she realized they would have to deliver it alone.

"Calm down," Josey said to Cheryl.

"I can't calm down! I'm about to have a baby!"

"Call Marshall again," Vicki said to Shelly as she moved closer to the bed. The top of the baby's head was hairy.

"Can I push?" Cheryl said.

"Wait," Vicki said. "Wanda told us not to let you—"

Cheryl screamed.

"They've got Wanda," Shelly said, holding the phone.

"Let me talk to her," Josey said.

Vicki was glad someone else was taking

charge. She didn't want to be the one caring
for the baby. What if she dropped it? She had
heard stories of women giving birth in cabs,
police cars, and even grocery stores, but she
never thought she would see one born in a
secret hideout.

"Yes," Josey said, "we can see the top.
Okay. Uh-huh. All right."

Vicki stepped aside as Josey examined
Cheryl. Vicki put a hand on the girl's shoulder. The last contraction had passed, and
another was coming quickly.

"All right, she's ready to push," Josey said.

"I can?" Cheryl said with relief.

"Wanda says to wait until the next one
comes, then take a deep breath and push
through the contraction."

"I don't know what that means," Cheryl
said.

"I'll help you, honey, just relax until—"

"Here it comes!"

Vicki moved to the foot of the bed. When
the contraction began, Cheryl took a breath,
held it, and closed her eyes. Her face turned
red, and Josey told her to take another
breath, but the girl kept pushing. Vicki
looked down and saw the baby's head move
an inch forward.

This is really happening, Vicki thought.

"Shelly, get some of those sterile cloths," Josey said.

"I don't know what to do," Vicki said.

"Just help me encourage Cheryl," Josey said. "You're doing fine."

Vicki found herself breathing and pushing along with Cheryl, her heart beating like a drum. "You're doing great, Cheryl! Good girl! It won't be long now."

The contraction wound down and Cheryl sat back, panting like a dog. Josey wiped her forehead and held the phone to her ear as Wanda gave instructions.

Cheryl's eyes widened, and she clutched the bedsheet. "Here comes another one!"

With each gasp of air and each push, the baby's head moved farther forward. Suddenly, Vicki saw the face of the child.

"The head's out!" Josey cried into the phone.

Vicki studied the child. "Its face is blue. Maybe that's normal, but—"

"Here," Josey said, shoving the phone into Vicki's ear.

"Tell me what you see," Wanda said.

Vicki could hardly contain her emotion. She had known Cheryl for several months and had talked with her about the baby, but in all that time of feeling it move, it had all seemed so far away. Now, staring at the child's face, Vicki wiped away tears of joy.

"The little face is pointing up, toward the ceiling," Vicki said, "and its color is kind of blue-green, like the color of your veins, and it's got the cutest—"

"Okay, listen carefully. I want you to put your fingers near the baby's neck. Don't let Cheryl push. Just feel the baby's neck and tell me if there's anything there. Hurry."

Vicki used both hands and felt around the baby's neck. "Yeah, there's something here."

"What's it feel like?"

"I don't know. It's kind of like a big, fat worm. Kind of squishy."

"That's what I was afraid of."

"What?"

"Vicki, we don't have much time. That thing around the baby's neck is the umbilical cord. We have to move it fast."

"How?"

"We need to reduce the pressure by easing the cord over the baby's head."

"I don't think I can—"

"You have to," Wanda pleaded. "It may already be too late, but you have to try."

"Okay, but how?"

"Grab the cord with your fingers."

"I'm trying, but I don't want to hurt—"

"Hurry, Vicki! See if you can pull the cord toward you. Does it move?"

"It's slippery."

"What's going on?" Cheryl said. "Is the baby okay?"

"Lie back and rest," Josey said.

"Can you pull it?" Wanda said.

"Yeah, it came forward a few inches, but that's all—"

"Good. That might be enough. Now I want you to take the cord and lift it over the baby's head. Just pull it over right now."

Vicki strained as she grasped the cord. "It's really tight. I'm afraid it's going to—"

"It won't break. Just pull it over. Did you do it?"

"No, it's stuck."

"You have to push it to the other side right now. I don't care how you do it—"

"—this is so scary!"

"—just do it!"

"Please, God," Vicki prayed, "please, God, please, God, please, God!"

Vicki took a step to her left and used both hands. With the cord tight against the top of the baby's head, she managed to ease it over and down toward its left shoulder. The child kept its eyes closed and didn't move.

"I need to push again!" Cheryl said.

"Is the cord over the head?" Wanda said.

"Yeah, I got it."

"Then tell her to push."

"Go ahead and push," Vicki said.

While Cheryl bore down again, Wanda spoke into Vicki's ear. "Get ready for the little thing to come out pretty quickly. It'll be sort of slick and a little bloody, but you'll be okay. Have someone there get a pair of sharp scissors or a knife and some shoestrings."

"Shoestrings?"

"Don't ask questions. Just do it."

"Take another deep breath," Josey said to Cheryl.

Vicki asked Shelly to get the scissors and more cloths as one of the baby's shoulders came out. Vicki kicked off her shoes and quickly removed the laces as she watched the baby's progress. "How will we know if the baby's okay?"

"Let's just get it out of there first," Wanda said.

Vicki took two of the cloths and held them in front of her. She felt like her dad, who played catcher for their church's softball team. With another push from Cheryl, the baby came sliding out, hands wiggling toward the ceiling. Vicki held the child gingerly, overwhelmed at the sight.

"It's a boy!" Josey said.

"Really?" Cheryl said, sitting up to have her first look at the child. "It's really a boy?"

"Don't hold the baby too low," Wanda said to Vicki. "Hold him about the same height as the bed where the mother is. That way we'll keep the blood flow even."

"Okay," Vicki said. "Now what?"

"Wipe the baby off, and don't hold him like a piece of china. Hold him like you know what you're doing."

Shelly brought scissors while Josey tied Vicki's shoelaces tightly at two spots on the cord.

"Why isn't he crying?" Vicki said.

"Cut the cord," Wanda said.

It took Vicki two tries to cut the umbilical cord. Blood splattered the floor.

"Is something wrong?" Cheryl said.

Josey kept the phone to Vicki's ear as Vicki cleaned the boy off. "Wanda, he's still blue— he's not crying."

"You need to clear the airway," Wanda said. "It could be mucus."

"What do I do?"

"Open his mouth a little and swab it out. Just put your finger in there."

Vicki put her finger near the boy's mouth. The child looked like a doll with his tiny lips and perfect fingers. His nose was flat, but

Vicki knew that would change. She cleaned some clear liquid from the child's mouth and held him up with both hands. "Please, God!"

"Now stroke his back with your hand," Wanda said. "Not too hard, but hard enough to get his little lungs going."

Cheryl leaned over and nearly fell out of bed. "Is he going to be okay? Tell me he's going to be all right."

Vicki glanced at Josey. Tears welled in the woman's eyes.

"It's not working," Vicki said, rubbing the baby's back.

"Okay, tip the baby's head back a little to open his airway. His chin should point to the ceiling. Now I want you to do this gently. Vicki, do you understand?"

"Yes, gently." Vicki held the baby in the crook of her left arm and tipped his head back. The child's mouth opened slightly.

"I want you to put your mouth over the baby's nose and mouth and gently blow. Just once, and don't do it hard, very gently."

"Please, God." Vicki placed her lips over the baby's nose and mouth and gave a puff of air. The child's throat gurgled, and Vicki felt his chest move slightly. He arched his back, squinted, and opened his mouth wide.

"What's happening?" Cheryl said.

Before Vicki could answer, a tiny, bubbling

cry echoed through the cabin. Vicki shook with emotion. It was the most wonderful sound she had ever heard.

"Oh, thank you, thank you, thank you."

"I heard that," Wanda whooped on the phone. "My watch says 2:23. That'll be the official time of birth, Dr. Vicki."

"Thank you so much for what you did," Vicki sobbed.

"It wasn't me, young lady," Wanda said. "You did everything I asked and more. Congratulations."

"What now?"

"We'll want to keep the baby warm. Unwrap him and put him on the mother's chest, skin to skin. Then cover them with blankets and cloths. The baby may want to nurse, that's good. Also, find something for the baby's head, like a little cap. Most of the heat is lost through the head."

Vicki handed the baby to Cheryl, and the girl snuggled him as Shelly covered them. Wanda gave instructions, and Josey and Shelly cleaned the room.

Vicki answered a knock at the door. Conrad stood with tears in his eyes. "We were listening out here and praying for you. I can't believe what you did."

"Thanks," Vicki whispered.

Charlie stepped forward. Phoenix was just behind him, wagging his tail and whining. "I found some pictures of little babies on the Internet and every one had a little cap on."

Charlie handed Vicki the tops of some floppy, white socks he had cut with scissors and decorated with markers. There were crude stars, moons, and some pictures Vicki couldn't identify.

"Those are the wise men coming to the baby Jesus," Charlie said. "I thought that would be good to put on his first hat."

"It's perfect," Vicki said.

She closed the door and pulled the covers back. The baby slept as she placed the floppy hat on his head and leaned down to kiss the child. "You're lucky you have a lot of people who were praying for you, little guy."

"He's lucky he had you taking care of him," Cheryl said, glowing with joy.

"I'll bet you're glad that's over," Vicki said.

"I'm so thirsty and hungry too."

Josey brought some fruit, water, and bread, and Cheryl ate with her eyes closed. Every few moments she pulled the covers back and looked into the face of her son. "I can't imagine what God must have gone through, giving up Jesus on the cross."

The door opened and Josey led her husband, Tom, into the room. The man smiled at Vicki, then quietly crept to Cheryl's bedside. "I heard it got pretty rough in here."

Cheryl smiled. "Nothing we couldn't handle." She pulled the bundle out from under the covers, and the baby's hat flopped in front of his face. Josey tried to stop her, but Cheryl shifted in the bed, then handed the boy to Tom.

Tom Fogarty was speechless. Josey looked over his shoulder and smiled, pulling the hat out of the boy's face. The child's eyelids scrunched tightly together, and Vicki noticed little white spots, like pimples, on his small, flat nose.

"Mr. Fogarty, I want you to meet your son, Ryan Victor."

"My son?"

"And let Mom hold him when you're finished," Cheryl said.

Vicki hugged Cheryl and wept. She couldn't wait to call Judd and tell him the good news.

FIVE

Dr. Rose

JUDD's mind raced as he prowled through the neighborhood, running away from the safe house. The believers who had helped him and Lionel were either dead or on the run—he knew that from the Peacekeepers' conversation.

"God, I don't know what to do," Judd prayed. "Give me some kind of sign."

He stayed away from streetlights while he walked, wondering when someone would discover him. He was a marked man without the tattoo of Carpathia and instant cash for any citizen who caught him.

Judd walked more than a mile until he came to a main road leading to town. He and Lionel had avoided such places the past few months, but now he knew he had to take the risk.

He spotted a blue sign with an *H* in the middle. Medical help. No matter what he did for Lionel, it would be worthless to simply get him out from under the rock without treating his arm. A plan slowly formed in Judd's mind as he ran toward the hospital.

※

Lionel awoke to a chirping noise. At first he thought it was some kind of bird, maybe a vulture. Then he realized it was the cell phone and smiled.

The night had turned colder, and in his sleep Lionel had tucked his right arm under him for warmth and had drawn his legs up toward his body. A soft breeze blew through trees, and Lionel smelled rain. *Great, that's all I need. The stream will rise and I'll drown.*

Lionel grabbed the phone on the third ring and answered.

"Lionel? It's Vicki."

Vicki's voice cheered him, and Lionel explained that Judd had left the phone and had gone for help.

"How are you?" Vicki said. "Judd told me a little about what happened."

"There's not much to tell. I've got this big rock on my arm, and I can't move. I've had a couple of animal visitors in the night, but that's about all. How's Cheryl?"

"She's doing well. She had the baby." Vicki described what had happened with Ryan Victor.

Lionel was astonished. "Hey, if you can deliver a baby and save his life, you could probably help me out. You want to come down here?"

"You don't know how much I'd give to do that. Are you in a lot of pain?"

"Only when I move." Lionel smiled, then thought about Chang's news of the safe house raid. He decided not to worry Vicki. "I'm really cold, but as soon as Judd gets back I'll be fine."

Vicki paused. "What if Judd doesn't come back?"

"He wouldn't leave me here."

"I know, and I don't want to think about this, but what if he runs into trouble? There's enough GC and vigilantes to catch all of us."

"Is this your way of cheering me up? I don't think Florence Nightingale would have done it this way."

Vicki chuckled, then grew serious. "I'm saying this for your own good. You have to think about what to do in the worst case."

"You don't understand. There's nothing I

can do. God's going to have to swoop down and roll this stone away, preferably not on the rest of me."

"Maybe there's somebody else in the area you could call."

"Yeah, I'll just try the Yellow Pages. Come on, Vicki. I'm stuck. The only other thing I could do is get my pocketknife out and . . ."

"What?"

"Nothing. I was just trying to be funny."

"I had Conrad put out a message on the Web site—"

"No. I don't want to alert the GC."

"We didn't give your location. We just put out an SOS so people could pray." The phone began to break up. "Looks like the phone is running low. It'll recharge once the sun comes out. I'll call you the minute I hear anything from Judd. Okay?"

"All right. But call me at first light."

Lionel hung up and put his head back on the ground. He reached for his arm and found the blood crusted and dry. That was the good news. The bad news was that everything was swollen. Lionel knew he risked infection, but he had no medicine and no way to treat the wound.

The conversation with Vicki had given him an idea, as far-fetched as it seemed. He could use his pocketknife—

No, things would have to get a lot worse for him to consider that.

Lionel set his jaw and closed his eyes. Judd was coming back. He would find a way to get the rock off, treat his wound, and they would keep going. He might lose the use of that arm, but he'd rather be alive than dead.

Judd would come back. That was the plan, and Lionel chose to believe it. Judd had to come back.

The hospital was a series of buildings that had survived the wrath of the Lamb earthquake. It was nearly 4 A.M. when Judd reached the darkened parking lot. He noticed a section for staff and saw a row of expensive autos. These were no doubt doctors' vehicles, and at the end, taking up two parking spaces, was a sleek-looking Humvee. The thing had to cost more Nicks than all the nurses were paid in a year.

Judd looked for a security camera but didn't see one. He spotted a night watchman at the front of the emergency room and carefully tiptoed to the back of the first building. He had no plan, other than to somehow get help for Lionel. The sight of the Humvee made him think the vehicle might have a jack that would lift the rock, but how would he get medicine?

Judd peeked in a window in the back and saw a nurse in scrubs at a small desk. The blinds were pulled at the next few windows. Then Judd came upon a patient room with two beds. Only one was occupied.

The door opened and a man who looked to be in his late thirties entered. He pulled the chart at the end of the bed, looked it over, then examined the male patient. "I'd say you were pretty lucky tonight," the doctor said, shining a light in the man's eyes. "Those Judah-ites can be pretty ornery."

"Yeah, and to think there was a nest of them right in our own town," the patient said.

"I think this knock on your head's nothing to worry about, but we're going to keep you a few more hours. I'm headed out, but Dr. Parker will be here in a few minutes. He'll take care of you."

Judd ducked as the doctor left the room. If the shift was changing, doctors and nurses would be going home. Judd made a quick decision and headed for the parking lot.

Vicki heard the van and snapped awake. Wanda was inside the cabin examining

Cheryl and the baby before Vicki wiped the sleep from her eyes. Wanda was older, with graying hair and a sagging face. There were bags under her eyes, and wrinkles everywhere, but there was something fresh about her—she seemed to light up the room as she did her work. Cheryl pointed at Vicki and Wanda turned, the mark of the true believer on the woman's forehead.

"So this is the young lady with the future in medicine," Wanda said, smiling and hugging Vicki. She kissed Vicki's cheek and took a step back. "You're a pretty little thing. You're sure you didn't go to medical school?"

Vicki giggled. "I actually didn't even make it out of high school."

"Well, you did excellent work with Cheryl and Ryan. Both look like they'll be fine. He came a little early and doesn't weigh much, but if he eats right, he should fill out in no time. He's also a little jaundiced."

Vicki furrowed her brow. "What's that?"

"It's common. You can tell by the skin. See, it's yellow. Best thing to do is put Ryan in the sunlight and let him sleep. You don't want him to get burnt, but the sun's rays start . . . well, all you need to know is that he needs to be in the sun a couple of hours a day."

Vicki yawned and Wanda told her to get

some sleep. "I'll still be here when you wake up."

"Good," Vicki said. "I have a lot of questions, and I'd love to hear your story. We don't get many visitors, except for the ones who come to see Zeke."

Wanda smiled. "Get some rest."

Judd found a small piece of pipe on the ground and slid under the Humvee, watching from the shadows as a few workers exited the hospital. He was careful not to touch the car and set off an alarm. He waited nearly thirty minutes, watching cars arrive and people in uniforms rush inside. Just as he was about to give up, the Humvee chirped and the engine started.

Judging from the shoes and the way the person walked toward the vehicle, Judd guessed it was a man. Maybe a doctor. When the man came around the back of the vehicle, Judd scooted out and caught up to him as the door opened. The man wore a white jacket and had a stethoscope draped around his neck.

"Hey," Judd said as he sprang from the shadows.

The man threw his hands in the air. "My

wallet's in my back pocket. I've only got about fifty Nicks but you can have—"

"Put your hands down. I don't want your money. Get in."

The man turned slowly. "Look, buddy, don't shoot. If you're looking for drugs—"

"Don't turn around. Just get inside. I don't want to hurt you."

After the man got inside, Judd opened the back door quickly and slid in. "We're driving out of here and to the back of the hospital, not past the guard, got it?"

"Yeah, but I hope you don't want me to go inside. You can't get in that way."

Judd knew Lionel needed medicine, but there was no way he could enter through the front. Judd's eyes landed on the rearview mirror. The man stared at Judd, the mark of Carpathia clear on his forehead. It was the same doctor he had seen through the window.

"Tell me what you want. Maybe I can help."

"A friend of mine's hurt. His arm is trapped under a rock."

"Where?"

"I can't tell you his location—"

"No, where on the arm?"

"Just below the elbow. The rock's huge. I put a tourniquet on him to stop the bleeding."

"How long has he been there?"

Judd looked at his watch. "A few hours."

"And he was conscious when you left him?"

"Yeah, he was talking, and I told him I'd be back before sunup."

The man put the vehicle in gear and backed out.

"Hey, where are you going?" Judd said.

"Duck your head so the guard doesn't see you. The windows are tinted, but if you pass a lighted area people can still see inside. I have some medical supplies at my house. We'll go there and then to your friend."

Judd shoved the pipe into the back of the seat. "Okay, but remember I have this."

The doctor drove by the guard, and Judd relaxed a little. He was tired, hungry, and thirsty.

"Looks like you have a few scratches yourself," the doctor said. "Anybody look at those?"

"I'm okay."

"Patrick Rose," the doctor said, reaching back.

Judd hesitated, then shook the man's hand. "I'm Judd."

The doctor glanced back, and Judd pulled away.

"Look, I can tell you're not a hoodlum. I don't think you're going to rob me, and I believe your story about your friend, so relax. I'm going to help you."

"What are you going to do?"

"We'll get some meds, then find him."

"Does this car have a jack?"

"I'm sure it does, but I've never seen it. The dealer sends someone out if I blow a tire, but I've only had this a few months. You can look for the jack while I get my black bag."

"I'll be going with you into the house."

"Suit yourself."

"Are you married?" Judd said.

The doctor raised his left hand. He wore no ring. "Not anymore. I lost my wife a few years ago."

They drove through a residential area and came to a house with an unattached garage. Dr. Rose stopped the car and held up his hands. Judd told him to put his hands down and stepped in behind him.

Traces of light shone on the horizon as the man put a key in the front door and opened it. Judd followed, looking at the gourmet kitchen with pots and pans hanging from the ceiling. Counters glistened when Dr. Rose hit the light switch. The refrigerator looked big enough to hold food for an army.

Judd was distracted and didn't hear the

soft padding of feet down the hall. Dr. Rose turned, smiling. "I want you to meet Princess."

Something growled in the hallway, and a huge dog stepped into the light.

Six

Princess

Judd took a step back and stared at the dog. It was a Great Dane mix and looked like a horse. The dog snarled, the hair on its back standing up straight. Judd had confronted dogs before, but he had never faced an animal this big.

"If I were you, I'd take your hands out slowly and stay very still," Dr. Rose said. "Princess doesn't like unannounced company. In fact, she doesn't like company at all."

"I have a gun," Judd said shakily.

"No, you have a pipe. I saw it in the car. Now drop it or I'm going to order Princess to—"

At the sound of her name, Princess perked up her ears and Judd interrupted the man. "No! Don't say it." The pipe clanged on the polished, wooden floor.

The dog sniffed the pipe and nudged it with her nose. Judd remained still, glancing at the back door.

"Sit down," Dr. Rose said. "Slowly. I'll get you something to eat. You up for eggs? I make a mean omelette."

"I don't have time. I have to get back to my friend."

Dr. Rose opened the refrigerator and pulled out some food. In a few moments he had the burners going and was whipping eggs in a metal bowl.

"I noticed you don't have the mark," Dr. Rose said. Judd sat silently watching Princess. "That could mean you've had no contact with civilization for a while, or it could mean you're an enemy of the Global Community. A Judah-ite, perhaps."

"I'll never take Carpathia's mark."

Dr. Rose mixed ingredients and poured eggs into a hot skillet. The smell of food cooking seemed like heaven, but Judd was prepared to jump and run.

"You'll eventually die, you know. They'll catch you and lop off your head."

"Carpathia's mark means a worse death than they could ever put me through."

Dr. Rose pushed the omelette onto a plate and put it in front of Judd. He noticed Princess had turned her attention to the eggs, thick drops of saliva running from both jowls. Dr. Rose fixed another omelette, cut off a large chunk, and tossed it to Princess. She caught it and swallowed it with one gulp.

"It keeps her coat nice and shiny," Dr. Rose said.

Judd felt guilty about eating, but the food looked so good and he was so hungry that he dived in. Nothing had ever tasted better.

The man opened the refrigerator and pulled out a carafe of orange juice. Because of Judd's life in the underground, he hadn't tasted juice for a long time. The sweet drink stung his stomach as he drained the glass.

"So, are you a Judah-ite?"

"What difference does it make? If I don't have the mark you can take me to the GC and get your reward."

Dr. Rose glanced around the kitchen. "Does it look like I need money?"

"You're not going to turn me in?"

Dr. Rose took a mouthful of food and sat back. "I became a doctor so I could help people. And I've never been impressed with Nicolae, though he did bring sanity when the world fell apart. Coming back from the dead was nothing short of a medical miracle, but I can see through the act."

"You don't think Nicolae is god?"

"Maybe he is. Maybe he isn't. At the end of the day, it doesn't do much for my patients. Which brings us to your friend."

Judd glanced out the window as the sun rose through the clouds.

Lionel shielded his face from the light rain with his hand. He had finally gotten more comfortable when the soft pattering of drops struck his face. He pulled the backpack over his face as the rain came harder.

Lionel's watch was on his left wrist, beneath the rock. He had the urge several times in the night to check the time, and he had even tried to look at it before remembering he couldn't.

Lionel glanced behind him and saw the cell phone in a puddle of water. He grabbed it, tried to dry it off, and stuck it in the backpack. He wanted to call Vicki, but that would have to wait.

Lionel thought again about the fox and the snake. Had that been a dream? It had seemed so real, but he knew his mind could play tricks.

"God," Lionel prayed, "I know Judd would have come back if he could, so he's either trying to get to me, or the GC have him. I trust you to help him. You are our strength."

Lionel thought about his prayer. God was his *strength.* It would take God's power to move the stone. *Unless . . .*

Maybe the reason God hadn't sent an angel or brought Judd back was because God wanted Lionel to act. Did God want to show his strength through Lionel's weakness?

Lionel reached in his pocket and pulled out the knife. It was the one his father had given him as a birthday present when he was thirteen. The bounty hunters in South Carolina almost took it away, but he managed to get it back. Lionel opened the main blade and ran his finger along the edge. Was it sharp enough?

"God, I need you to make it clear whether I should wait for Judd or do something else."

Judd couldn't understand why Dr. Rose was acting like a friend. Could Judd trust anyone with the mark of Carpathia? The man's eternal destiny was sealed, so there was no sense explaining the truth of God and the Bible. And yet, the man didn't seem concerned that Judd was an enemy of the Global Community.

Judd explained Lionel's injury, and with each bit of information Dr. Rose became more concerned. Judd told him about the tourniquet and what his arm looked like.

"He needs attention right now," Dr. Rose said, "but I don't think trying to lift that rock is going to do much. You may have saved his life with the tourniquet, but if he's exposed for too long, things could get bad."

"He could lose the arm?"

"He's already lost it. The question is whether the rest of him will survive."

Judd felt sick. Lionel's injury was Judd's fault. If only he hadn't sat on that boulder.

"I'll get my stuff and you can show me the way," Dr. Rose said.

"Why are you helping me? You're just endangering yourself, and for what?"

"I figure, if you've made it this far, and if you're willing to risk your life for your friend, you deserve a chance. The GC may catch you. That's none of my business. My job is to help anybody I find who's hurt."

Judd stared into the man's eyes. *What other choice do I have?*

"I'll get my stuff and meet you in the car."

Judd stood from the table and froze as Princess growled.

"Princess, sit," Dr. Rose said.

The dog sat.

"Princess, friend."

The dog cocked his head, and Dr. Rose said the word *friend* again. To Judd's surprise, Princess stood on her hind legs, put her front paws on Judd's shoulders, and licked his face.

A few minutes later, Judd and the doctor were in the Humvee, heading for the woods. Judd asked to use the man's phone and dialed Lionel. It rang but there was no answer.

Dr. Rose turned on the radio to a GC report of a midnight raid on Judah-ites. He quickly switched it off.

"Before we got to your house, you mentioned you had a wife," Judd said, breaking the silence. "What happened to her?"

"She disappeared. She was carrying our first child."

"Were you with her at the time?"

Dr. Rose shook his head. "I was at the hospital. The whole place was crazy that night. Women with babies disappearing from their wombs. Patients freaking out because their roommates had vanished. Nurses were gone. The security guard's clothes were in a pile outside the emergency room.

"We started getting accident victims after that. Car accidents, that kind of thing. I called the house in the morning, but there was no answer. I figured my wife had gone to see her family, but they didn't answer either. I got home about three the next afternoon. Her car was in the garage, but she wasn't at the house. I finally found her nightgown in the bed upstairs. She was gone."

"What do you think happened?"

Dr. Rose shook his head. "I've heard all the theories, but it doesn't matter. They're not coming back."

"I know where they are."

Dr. Rose rolled his eyes. "Are you sure you want to risk preaching to me? I might turn you in."

Judd pointed the way past the safe house.

After a few moments the doctor turned. "All right, tell me. Where do you think they are?"

"First, I'll guess about your wife. She was religious, right?"

"Not until the last few months."

"Something happened that changed her, and she wanted you to change too."

Dr. Rose shrugged. "I guess you could put it that way."

"And the same thing happened to her family."

"Her mom and dad were already religious wackos. Teri just bought into it a little late. How did you know?"

"It fits," Judd said. "It's because they

believed the same thing about Jesus that they were taken."

"Right. And if you know all this, why are you still here?"

"My family was taken just like your wife and unborn baby."

"I'm sorry."

"I'd heard about God all my life. I never really took it seriously. Now I'm trying to tell as many as I can about the truth."

"What truth?"

"That God loved you enough to die for you. That he made a way to come to him through his Son, Jesus."

"Yeah, Teri listened to a Jesus station on the radio," Dr. Rose said, furrowing his brow. "So what happens to us? Will we ever see them again?"

Judd pursed his lips. "Those who accept the gift God offers will see those who disappeared again. That's one of God's promises."

Dr. Rose slammed on his brakes and slid to the right. Judd wore a seat belt, but he still went flying forward.

"That's what frosts me about you people. You're so sure about everything, and it's all in the future. Someday you'll do this, and someday God's going to make everything better. At least Carpathia does stuff for us right now."

"Carpathia is the enemy of God. Those who follow him and take his mark—"

"What? They don't have a chance at your little after-death party?" He shifted and pulled back onto the road.

Judd recognized the street and some of the buildings. They were close to the turnoff where they would find Lionel. Judd didn't want to anger the doctor, but he didn't feel right about keeping quiet. "I'm telling you straight what I believe. I don't want you to get mad and turn me into the GC—"

"If I wanted to do that, believe me, your head would already be rolling on the ground." He paused. "What's your Bible say about me?"

Judd took a breath. "Taking the mark of Nicolae and worshiping his image means you've made your choice."

Dr. Rose gritted his teeth, but before he could speak, his beeper went off. He studied the number as he drove. "This could be a problem."

He pulled the Humvee to the roadside and dialed a number. "This is Dr. Rose. . . . Yes . . . okay, but listen, I'm on an emergency. . . . No, I understand. I'll be right there." He threw the car into gear and made a U-turn, cutting off an oncoming car.

"What's going on?"

"Emergency at the hospital. Some rebels ambushed a high-ranking GC official. They need me to patch him up."

"Can't somebody else do it?"

"Head of the hospital picked me and wouldn't take no for an answer."

"What about Lionel?"

"So that's his name, huh? Lionel will have to hold out until we can get to him." Dr. Rose scowled. "Of course, if we don't get to him in time, God'll just take him to heaven, right?"

SEVEN

Lionel's Battle

LIONEL pulled the phone from his backpack and dialed Vicki. He needed to talk through his options with someone he loved. The phone was still wet, and Lionel couldn't see the readout on the phone's face.

"Must need more of a charge," Lionel said, placing the phone on the ground. A cloud moved and the sun peeked through, but the phone was still in the shadow of the rock.

Lionel put his head back. His whole body ached. He had read the verse about Christians being members of a body, and that if one member hurt, the others did too. Lionel felt that verse with his back, neck, and ankle that he had hurt trying to get out of the rock's way. His right hand was scraped and crusted with blood. His hair felt like it was full of ants, though Lionel couldn't tell if bugs were really crawling on him or not.

Lionel pushed the phone as far away as he could, but he couldn't reach the sunshine. *Soon,* Lionel thought, *the sun will move this way and I'll call Vicki.*

Lionel had to think clearly. If Judd didn't return, what would he do? How long could he survive on the food and water left? And how long could he last if the sun beat down on him all day? He looked around for the second sandwich and unwrapped it.

Lionel remembered how his mom cut the edges from his sandwiches when he was little. Now, with his stomach growling, he devoured the crust. He made a quick inventory of his food and found one more sandwich, packages of crackers and potato chips, and a few cookies. He had four small bottles of water. That was enough to keep him going through the day. Judd would be back by evening unless . . .

Lionel watched a cotton-candy cloud float through the sky. He closed his eyes and looked again, studying the shape. It looked like a face, with two eyes and a nose. Suddenly, Lionel saw Nicolae Carpathia's face, the old devil himself looking down. Nicolae looked like he was laughing.

Lionel closed his eyes. More than ever, he

knew he was in a battle. From the moment
Lionel had prayed to accept Jesus as Lord and
Savior, he had stepped into a war, not of
flesh and blood, but an unseen battle of
good versus evil. Lionel had sensed it early.
Satan and his followers must have loved it
that Lionel lied to his parents about his faith,
but after the disappearances, Lionel knew he
had to respond to the truth of the Bible. That
decision hurtled him into a daily struggle
against the forces of evil.

But Lionel knew no matter how fierce the
battle, he was on the winning side. The evil
one would try to get him to fight with his
own friends, whisper things to get him to
doubt, but Lionel had to follow God and
listen to him.

Lionel opened his eyes. The cloud was
gone and he was glad. He looked around but
saw no sign of the fox or snake. The rippling
stream was soothing, but he also realized he
had to go to the bathroom.

A rumbling stirred the peaceful scene. An
engine revved. Was he imagining this or was
it real?

Judd remained silent on the trip back to the
hospital. He thought about asking the doctor

to let him out, but someone would spot him in broad daylight. Judd said a quick prayer and ducked as Dr. Rose pulled into the parking lot. The man turned off the engine and took the keys from the ignition. "I don't suppose it'd be smart of you to go inside with me."

"Unless you want to get me killed."

Dr. Rose sighed. "Look, I'm sorry about your friend. I'll try to make this quick. Will you stay here?"

Judd nodded.

Dr. Rose handed him the keys. "Use these if you need to put the windows down. Don't take the car. I'll report you if you do, and the GC will be on you." He got out and hurried toward the hospital.

Judd sat quietly in the backseat, watching the emergency entrance and counting the number of GC cruisers. All Dr. Rose had to do was tell one Peacekeeper and Judd was toast. He didn't like trusting anyone who wasn't a believer, but there was something about this man that made Judd think he wouldn't turn him in.

Judd wished he could call Vicki. He had promised to get in touch, but Lionel needed the phone more. Judd opened the glove compartment, pulled out the owner's manual, and found a diagram that led him to a storage compartment in the back. He studied the jack, wondering if it would move the giant rock.

Judd put the jack in the backseat and waited. *Am I doing the right thing staying here?*

※

Vicki awoke around 9 A.M. and asked if anyone had called. Shelly shook her head. Vicki tried dialing Lionel but got a weird ring.

The baby, Ryan Victor, was sleeping when Vicki peeked in on him. Wanda had examined him and trimmed his cord. Cheryl was sleeping, so Vicki held the baby. Wanda paced the room, and Vicki asked if something was wrong.

"The baby's fine," Wanda whispered. "Really healthy, even though he's a little early. He's nursing and getting enough to eat. I'm concerned about the mother. The birth took a lot out of her. If she were in a hospital they'd have given her an IV with lots of fluid. She can't stay awake long enough to eat or drink anything."

"What could that be?"

"Might be that she's just tired. I'm hoping that's all it is and that we'll get her through this." She put a hand on Vicki's shoulder. "You need to motivate her."

"I don't understand."

Wanda sat and patted the bench for Vicki to join her. The baby stuck out his tongue and made a sucking sound, then turned and went back to sleep.

"Cheryl has given the baby to the Fogartys, right?" Wanda said.

Vicki nodded.

"I've seen it happen before. If the mom is weak and something goes wrong, she can lose her will to keep going. For the baby's sake, you've got to help that girl take care of herself. Even if the Fogartys raise him, he's going to need his mother's milk. You can get formula on the black market, but it's pretty difficult to find."

Wanda took the baby from Vicki and explained more about what Vicki should do, and Vicki took notes. Finally, she asked how Wanda had become a believer.

"I was a nurse for a number of years. Then I trained couples about the birthing process. You know, breathing techniques, that stuff. I even went with couples to the hospital and stayed with them when the baby came."

"What made you want to do that?"

"My father was a doctor. He used to talk about the miracle of birth, how every one of them was a gift from God. Delivering babies interested me, but I didn't think God had anything to do with it.

"One night I was helping a couple who had gone through a difficult pregnancy. The mother had been on bed rest for weeks, and the labor was going way into the night. The doctor finally decided they had to do a C-section."

"That's where they operate on the mom?"

"Right. I was there when they took her to surgery. The doctor did a perfect procedure. All the monitors said both the mother and baby were fine. The doctor made the last cut, put both hands around the baby, and lifted her out. I saw the little one's face. The doctor looked at the mother and said, 'You have a beautiful baby girl.' Then the doctor's hands flew into the air, and the baby's umbilical cord dropped to the floor. That child had simply disappeared before our eyes."

"It must have been awful."

Wanda nodded. "The mother started screaming, asking what they had done with the baby. One of the nurses fainted.

"That's when I started thinking more about God and what my father had said. I read my Bible, but it didn't make much sense. I found some answers on the Internet and prayed a prayer they listed. I kept working at the hospital until the wrath of the Lamb earthquake, and then I moved up here to get away from the GC. God brought several pregnant moms to me, and I got sort of a reputation. I'm glad to still be part of bringing little ones into the world, but I have to tell you I don't know what kind of world it's going to be."

"It would be a lot worse for us if you weren't in it."

Wanda cradled the baby and hummed an old hymn. "I used to think my parents were crazy for believing all that stuff about Jesus coming back. I just wish it hadn't taken all that's happened to convince me."

Lionel raised his head as far has he could, shielding his eyes from the sun with his hand. He pushed the bottles of water and food under the rock to keep them cool.

The engine revved again. *Could it be Judd? Maybe he's forgotten the way.*

Lionel listened as the rumbling stopped, and then he heard voices. Perhaps Judd had made it to the safe house and had gotten help before the GC raid.

Someone whistled and a dog barked. Then another. Lionel's heart sank. He was trapped and the GC was closing in.

Judd rested in the backseat of the Humvee. When it got too hot, he cracked the windows a few inches to let in some fresh air. Throughout the morning, Judd listened to conversations of people passing. Some talked about the expensive vehicles, upset that doctors made so much money. Most discussed their work or things at home.

". . . and it was all over the news about the Judah-ites they caught last night," one woman said.

"I didn't hear about it until this morning," another answered, "but I'm not surprised. There were a lot of them around before the GC started the mark of loyalty, and then they just disappeared. . . ."

Every few minutes, Judd glanced at the hospital to make sure the GC weren't coming for him. He had scouted his escape route if someone came. Judd could jump out and run through a residential section or barrel away in the doctor's Humvee, but that would mean maneuvering out of the parking lot, which Judd didn't think he could do quickly.

He looked at his watch and tapped his foot. Dr. Rose was taking too long.

Lionel lay perfectly still, listening for any movement. He guessed the vehicle rumbling in the distance had stopped because of the trees a few hundred yards away. He hoped the rain had washed away their tracks, but the dogs worried him. Whoever was out there was looking for him or some other rebel.

Rebel. Lionel liked the word. He was a rebel, trying to free the captives. He was a child of the king, on a mission not just to save his own life but also to save others. But how long would he be a rebel?

"God, keep me safe right here," he prayed silently.

Judd was startled at the knock on the window. He had dozed off on the plush seats, and the car felt like it was one hundred degrees.

Dr. Rose opened the front door and hopped in, handing Judd a Styrofoam box. "Here's some lunch from the cafeteria. No guarantees."

Judd glanced at his watch. It was ten minutes after noon! "What took so long?"

"The GC had an accident. From what I can tell, it wasn't caused by rebels, but that's who they're blaming."

"How much longer you gonna be?"

Dr. Rose shook his head. "One of the guys still has internal bleeding. They want me to stay until everybody's stabilized."

Judd slammed the box of food on the seat. "And how long will that take?"

"I told you I don't know. Now you can get mad or work with me. I found out from one of the guys that there's a detail of GC with dogs looking for rebels north of town."

"That's where Lionel is."

"That's what I thought." Dr. Rose scratched his head. "You know, it might be best if they find him. They could bring him back here and let me—"

"You know the first thing they'll do to him," Judd said. "They'll take him to the guillotine. They won't waste a hospital bed for someone they're going to kill."

Dr. Rose got out of the car. "Eat something. I'll be back as soon as I can."

EIGHT

Lionel's Decision

LIONEL couldn't see movement above him, but he could hear the searchers getting closer. Radios squawked. A female laughed.

Small rocks skittered down the embankment, and Lionel closed his eyes. The men were right above him on top of the hill. His only chance now was to lay still and keep out of sight. The rock on his arm had trapped him, but it was also hiding him.

"Tell me again what we're supposed to be looking for," a man said with a drawl.

"You know they caught a bunch of Judahites under the old feed store," another man said.

"Yep."

"Well, before they took them to the guillotine one of the younger ones told the GC about a couple of guys heading north last night."

"So we're looking for two?"

"Yeah. One black, one white."

So the GC hasn't caught Judd, Lionel thought. *But where could he be?*

Several others joined the two at the top of the hill. A man with a nasally voice took control. From what he heard, Lionel guessed there were a few Peacekeepers and Morale Monitors along with volunteers.

"The dogs haven't picked up anything, but I'm not willing to give up," Nasal Voice said. "From the information we have, the two on the loose were Judah-ites, maybe high up in the so-called Tribulation Force. As you know, there's an extra bounty for those."

Lionel wondered who in the Salem group had talked. He felt sorry for the people who had faced the blade and couldn't blame them for giving information.

"My guess is, we're a little off their trail," Nasal Voice continued.

"Which way, sir?"

Lionel's heart pounded. If the group came down the hill, they would spot him. If they came to the stream they would see him too.

"Our best bet is to get back to the vehicles and push a little farther east where there aren't as many trees. We'll have helicopter support later in the afternoon."

"Maybe a few of us should follow that stream," a man said. "We could spread out—"

"I'll give the orders," Nasal Voice barked, "and we'll stick together and head east. I don't think the Judah-ites would have the guts to try to go through land like this. It's too hard."

Someone threw a rock that landed in the stream behind Lionel. It splashed with a loud *ka-thunk*. The group moved away, and Lionel sighed. They had missed him this time, but a helicopter would surely spot him. He picked up the phone and dialed Vicki's number.

💥

Judd watched the doctor go into the hospital, then opened the Styrofoam box. He found some cold French fries and an even colder grilled cheese sandwich. He shoved a few fries into his mouth, took a bite of the sandwich, and thought of Lionel. If he had remained conscious and hadn't lost too much blood, there was still a chance he was alive. But if the doctor was forced to stay at the hospital, Judd was out of ideas.

He pushed the food away, put his head on the seat in front of him, and prayed.

✳

Vicki was trying to get Cheryl to eat lunch when Shelly brought the phone. "Lionel wants to talk."

Vicki took the phone and walked to the other side of the room. Lionel sounded a little better than before, but something about his voice scared her. He explained what had happened since they last talked. The bleeding had stopped and Lionel felt stronger, but the prospect of the GC being in the woods along with the execution of his friends back at the hideout had terrified him.

"I wanted to talk to you before I go ahead with what I'm about to do," Lionel said.

"I don't understand," Vicki said.

"There's a verse somewhere in the New Testament. It's Jesus talking about it being better for a man to poke out his eyes than for his whole body to go to hell."

"Lionel, stop."

"I can't remember what Jesus was teaching there, but I figure it's better for me to be able to live without my arm than to stay here and die or get caught by the GC."

"Lionel—"

"Please, just listen. I know you care a lot about me. So I have to ask your help."

"I'd do anything for you, but—"

"It's my arm. I've got a pocketknife here, and I think it's sharp enough—"

"Stop it!"

"Vicki, I know it's hard to think about, but this might be my only chance. I have no idea where Judd is—I don't think the GC caught him, but I can't be sure. There's a chopper coming this afternoon, so if I don't get out, they're sure to see me, and you know what they'll do. I have no feeling in my left arm, and I think the bones were crushed."

Vicki felt woozy. Lionel was talking about something so horrible she could hardly listen. But this could be his only chance to live. She tried to put aside the sick feeling in her stomach. "All right. What do you need to know?"

"Is there anyone there who knows about medical stuff? I'm going to need help."

Vicki told him about Wanda. "Her specialty is babies. I'm not sure she could—"

"Put her on."

Vicki quickly explained the situation to Wanda. The woman took a breath and held a hand over the phone. "Even if he does this cleanly, he's going to have to get some medical treatment."

"There's not much chance of that," Vicki said.

"If someone doesn't clean the wound, he could get an infection and die. Plus, he needs—"

"If he doesn't get out, he's going to be dead anyway," Vicki said.

Wanda spoke with Lionel, asking him if he could see any blood or feel any broken bones. Vicki walked out of the cabin and called everyone together. It was time to pray.

※

Lionel talked with a woman he had never met, asking questions he never thought he would ask, about to do something he never dreamed of doing. In order to save his life, he was going to have to amputate his own arm.

He had heard of mountain climbers doing this, and he had even heard an old radio broadcast once about a man whose leg had been trapped by a falling tree. *It has been done before*, he told himself.

"There's no way you're going to cut through the bone with a pocketknife," Wanda said. "How is your arm positioned?"

"It's turned up, with the elbow pointing toward the ground."

"That's good. Now you're going to have to find a way around the bone. Can you reach your elbow with your right hand?"

Lionel reached under the rock as far as he could. "Just barely."

"Is the arm numb? Pinch yourself, or put the knife blade up to the skin below the tourniquet and see if you can feel anything."

Lionel preferred pinching himself. He used his fingernails but only felt slight pressure.

"All right," Wanda said. "I knew a hunter once who had to do this to his leg."

"What happened to him?"

"He wasn't being chased by the GC like you, but he lived. Last I heard he had taken up fishing." Wanda paused. "Lionel, how far are you from medical help?"

"I don't know. Probably a couple of hours from the town. But finding anybody who would take me in will be the problem."

"We'll pray. Now, if you're ready, I can try and walk you through this."

The clouds were gone, and the sun beat down on Lionel's face. The stream swelled with the night's rain and pushed the edges of its banks. A black bird flew overhead, and Lionel heard the familiar caw of the crow.

In order to perform the procedure, Lionel knew he would have to talk with Wanda, put the phone down, pick up the knife, and continue. "I've always wanted to be a doctor, so here goes."

*

Vicki couldn't bear hearing Wanda's instructions to Lionel, so she and the others gathered in the main cabin. Phoenix seemed to sense something was wrong, and he whined at the door. Before leaving to join Wanda, Marshall Jameson suggested they pray short, sentence prayers.

"Dear God," Charlie prayed, "I want to ask you to show Lionel exactly what he needs to do to get out from under that rock."

"And, Lord," Darrion continued, "help Wanda know what to say. Give her wisdom."

"Father," Mark said, "you know how much Lionel means to us. I pray you would give him your strength, through your Holy Spirit."

There was a pause, and Vicki heard a few sniffles around the room.

"I can't imagine what Lionel's going through right now," Shelly prayed, "but you are the Great Physician. You answered our prayers for Cheryl and baby Ryan, and now we pray you would help Lionel."

"Nothing happens without you knowing about it," Janie said. "It's hard to even think about, but we put our trust in you, and we give Lionel and his life to you."

Conrad slipped into the room and knelt with the others. When he caught his breath, he prayed, "Father, I know Lionel's started the operation. Guide his hand, and help Wanda and Marshall as they talk to him. Don't let him pass out, Lord, and keep the GC away."

Vicki felt overcome with emotion. She tried to remember the first time she had seen Lionel. She had heard about him from Lionel's older sister. Clarice had shared a seat on the school bus with Vicki, and Vicki had seen her family's picture, but the day after the disappearances was the first time she had actually met Lionel. She saw him first near New Hope Village Church, Lionel on his bike and Vicki on foot. Lionel had the same features as his sister, a cute face and round nose, but Vicki could tell the boy had been crying that day. They were both scared. Their family members had vanished.

As she thought of the emotion of that day, Vicki brushed a tear from her face and cleared her throat. "Father, I know that as much as we love and care for Lionel, you love him even more. You gave your only Son to die for him. So we ask you to comfort us with that love, and help us not be afraid."

"Give us the chance to help Lionel when he comes back to us," Zeke said.

"Yes, Lord."

"Amen."

Vicki put her head in her hands. Never had she heard the kids pray so strongly or more sincerely. Words came straight from the heart as they pleaded with God to spare Lionel. After a few minutes, the kids didn't pause between prayers, picking up from the last word and continuing in one long petition for Lionel's life. At one point, Josey Fogarty asked the kids to break into groups of two. The room came alive with voices, some shaking with emotion.

As the voices grew louder, the door opened. Vicki looked up and saw Wanda with the phone in her hand. Marshall walked in beside her. Neither smiled or gave a hint of what had happened.

Finally, with his chin trembling, Marshall said, "It's over."

Throughout the afternoon, Judd felt like he was going crazy. He watched for any sign of Dr. Rose, but he didn't return. Several times Judd reached for the door handle to leave or studied the keys, wondering if it was time to make a getaway, but something told him to wait.

Finally, as evening approached, a figure rushed through the emergency room exit and headed for the Humvee. Dr. Rose hopped in, and Judd threw him the keys. The man squealed his tires on the way out, waving and smiling at the scowling security guard.

"Did you hear anything from the GC about Lionel?" Judd said.

"I heard one Peacekeeper say there's a chopper out there, but I don't know if they found anything."

Judd sighed and rolled his window down a little to let fresh air in. "Thanks for not sending them to get me."

"Thank me when you find your friend."

For a second, Judd had the sinking feeling that the doctor was leading him into a trap. He dismissed the thought, knowing there was nothing he could do but try and get to Lionel as quickly as he could.

Judd gave the man directions and ducked when they saw someone on the street. A GC cruiser flashed his lights, and Dr. Rose cursed. "Get down in the back and don't say anything."

Judd held his breath as the doctor rolled down his window. He spoke angrily to the patrolman. "I just patched up three of your friends at the hospital—the least you can do is let me go home and get some sleep."

The man went back to his car, then returned, apologizing to the doctor and telling him to have a nice evening.

Dr. Rose pulled away and found the route Judd and Lionel had taken into the woods. Skirting trees and sometimes going over the small ones, the doctor was able to navigate the way in half the time it would have taken them to walk.

As the sun set, they came to an area near the woods with tire tracks. Judd found food wrappers in the dirt and assumed the GC had been there. He grabbed the tire jack and led the doctor to the stream. The two followed it until they came to the hill from the night before. It was the first time Judd had seen it in daylight, and the height of the incline took his breath away. He climbed over some smaller rocks and spotted the boulder that had fallen on Lionel.

"Would you mind waiting here?" Judd said.

"Go ahead."

Judd walked slowly, hoping his friend would still be alive. "Lionel?" he called out.

No answer.

"I brought some help," Judd continued.

"You don't have to worry about that helicopter or any of those Peacekeepers looking for you."

Judd reached the huge rock that held his friend, took a breath, and peeked around the corner. What he saw made him drop the jack and fall to his knees.

NINE

Getting Help

JUDD stared in disbelief. Lionel was gone—at least his body was gone. Judd turned away as Dr. Rose raced forward and knelt by the empty water bottles and blood.

"These are the kind of people you're following," Judd said with disgust. "They chopped off his arm so they could drag him away and cut off his head."

Dr. Rose scanned the area. "I don't think the GC did this."

"How can you defend them?"

"I'm not defending. Look at the ground. The only footprints here are yours and your friend's."

"Then how—?"

"Either somebody got here before us, or—"

"Or what?"

"Or he did this himself."

"That's impossible. Nobody would be able to . . ." Judd stopped when he remembered Lionel's pocketknife. The thought of Lionel cutting off his own arm to escape sickened him. He looked around for the backpack and the phone, but they were gone.

Dr. Rose followed some footprints and a trail of blood to the edge of the stream. "He's still losing a lot of blood. See the trail? Looks like he walked over to the stream to clean the wound."

"Is that bad?"

"Cleaning it's the right thing, but this water could cause an infection. We need to find him—fast."

Judd waded into the stream and searched for any footprints on the other side. "If there were dogs out here, he could have waded in to throw them off his trail."

A sound broke over the trickling of water, and Judd recognized the *thwock-thwock-thwock* of a helicopter. He instinctively ducked, but Dr. Rose pointed east. "They're over there."

Dr. Rose stumbled out of the stream and climbed up the other side of the bank. Judd followed, jumping out of the way of a small water snake. As the chopper moved farther away, the sound grew faint.

The light was fading, and Judd figured they had only a few more minutes of daylight. With their eyes glued to the ground, the two moved by the stream, looking for any sign of Lionel.

Nothing.

Judd was about to turn around and go the other way, but something in the woods caught his eye. "Lionel?" Judd whispered.

It was the most wonderful and terrible sight Judd had ever seen. The young man who had been with him since the start of the Young Tribulation Force—Lionel Washington, the strong, resourceful, solid, and steady member—stumbled out from behind a rock, his right arm held up in a wave, his shirt covered with blood. Judd's belt was still tightly wrapped around what was left of Lionel's left arm.

Judd rushed to his friend and grabbed him as Lionel collapsed.

"I didn't think you were coming back."

"Sorry it took me so long," Judd said through tears. "It's okay. We're here. This is Dr. Rose."

Dr. Rose examined Lionel's arm. "What did you do this with?"

"My pocketknife. A woman on the phone helped me. After I got away from the rock, I think I passed out. I don't know for how long."

"Is he going to be okay?" Judd whispered.

Dr. Rose ignored Judd's question, pulled out a light, and flashed it in Lionel's eyes. He asked Lionel a series of quick questions, then helped Judd carry him back across the stream. "We have to get to the car."

Lionel's head lolled back as they carried him. "You don't have the mark, Doctor. Why not?"

Dr. Rose looked at Judd. "He's not seeing clearly. That concerns me."

Judd winked at Lionel and whispered, "I'll explain in the car."

Lionel floated in and out of consciousness as Judd and Dr. Rose helped move him toward the car. His thoughts swirled in a sea of dull pain. What day was it? Why had this man with the mark of Carpathia come with Judd? Lionel reached to scratch his left hand, then realized it wasn't there.

As they walked along the wooded area he saw the fox. The animal licked its paws, turned its head, and was gone.

When they reached the car, Judd spread a blanket on the backseat and helped Lionel get settled. Dr. Rose handed him three pills. "These will ease the pain."

Lionel put the pills on his tongue and

washed them down with a gulp of water. He put his head on the seat and closed his eyes.

🌟

Judd wrapped Lionel's injured arm with a piece of fabric torn from a blanket, and Dr. Rose told him how to apply it. Judd pulled the pack off Lionel's back and looked inside. The bloody pocketknife lay at the bottom. Judd clenched his teeth and decided to leave it alone. Instead, he took the phone, also spattered with blood, and called Vicki.

"Lionel?" Vicki answered. "Is that you?"

"No, it's me, Vick. We've got him now."

"Oh, thank you, God!" Vicki said. Her voice muffled as she told the others Judd was calling. "Are you all right?"

"After seeing Lionel, I'll never complain again. I hear somebody with you helped him."

Vicki told Judd what had happened in Wisconsin, and Judd couldn't believe how God had answered their prayers. Judd explained that he had found a doctor who was going to help Lionel.

"A believer?" Vicki said.

"No. I can't explain right now."

"Judd, how do you know he's not going to take you to the GC and turn you over to them?"

"I don't know that for sure. I'm taking this one decision at a time."

"We'll be praying. Just let us know what happens."

Judd hung up and stashed the phone in his pocket.

Dr. Rose looked in the rearview mirror. "Who was that?" He put up a hand before Judd could answer. "Don't tell me. I don't want to know."

"Some friends of ours we're trying to get back to. It's been a long time."

"I'm not going to be able to take him to the hospital," Dr. Rose said. "First thing they do these days is check for the mark of Carpathia. I'll need to stop there and get some supplies though. Then we can head to my place."

Judd spent a few tense moments in the parking lot, wondering whether the doctor would bring the GC back with him, but the man returned alone, just like he said.

It was dark when they arrived at his house, and they quickly carried Lionel inside. Princess met them at the door and followed them downstairs where they placed Lionel on a pool table. Judd couldn't bear watching the doctor sew Lionel's wound, so he went to the kitchen and flipped on the television to catch up with the latest from the Global Community.

The world was still in awe of the miracle

workers. These false messiahs performed miraculous deeds for the sick, diseased, maimed, and disabled. One program featured a collection of video clips from around the world. After a miracle had been performed, the video made sure viewers knew this was all done by Nicolae's power.

Judd switched channels and found live coverage of yet another Z-Van concert. This time Z-Van had taken his crew into a remote country in Africa. As a camera panned the audience, Judd was surprised to see people with no mark on their foreheads. An announcer explained that because of technical difficulties with materials, many in this region had not been able to take Carpathia's mark.

Though people in the audience could not understand the man's words, Z-Van screamed his lyrics, pranced, danced, and flew over the stage. When he soared into the air with his demonic message, the crowd seemed mesmerized. A huge hologram of Nicolae appeared and spoke a message in the local language. Judd was about to turn the coverage off when a camera jerked wildly away from Z-Van and tilted. The producer quickly cut to another camera that focused on people in the crowd. Instead of enjoying Z-Van's show, they seemed upset, pointing at the sky and shrieking.

Finally, the screen showed a wide shot of the scene. Z-Van stood cowering on the stage. Musicians ran for their lives. A man stood several yards from the microphones, but it was clear everyone in the crowd heard him.

"My name is Christopher," the man said, "and I come to you on behalf of the true and living God."

Princess darted into the kitchen, the hair on her back standing on end.

Christopher explained the gospel and told people they should ask God's forgiveness for their sin. "That forgiveness is offered through God's only Son, Jesus Christ."

Another angel, Nahum, appeared next to Christopher and warned of the coming fall of Babylon. He urged people not to take the mark of Carpathia, that it would mean death to their souls. "Anyone who accepts the mark of the beast and worships his image seals their fate for all eternity."

"Accept the mercy of God now," Christopher said.

It was clear to Judd that people working behind the scenes were frantically trying to get the program off the air. Z-Van paced the stage like a caged lion, sneering at the angels who didn't seem to notice him. As Christopher led a prayer, people near the stage prayed and received the mark of the true believer. Judd closed his eyes and gave thanks that God was still working.

"What are you watching?" Dr. Rose said.

Judd stood, frightened by the voice. "Just a concert." He turned the TV off. *What do I talk with this man about now?*

Dr. Rose grabbed a beer from the refrigerator, popped the top, and leaned against the kitchen counter. "Your friend is pretty shaken. I cleaned and dressed the wound. It's not going to look as nice as if I'd done it at the hospital, but he'll live."

"Thanks. I-I know you took a risk helping us."

"That's what a doctor's supposed to do, right?"

"Not a loyal doctor for the Global Community. Your first duty is to help Nicolae rid the world of people like me."

Dr. Rose frowned. "Yeah, maybe I just added to the human pollution."

"Where should I go with him? We can't stay here."

"No, you can't." The man rubbed his eyes, and Judd remembered how long they had both been awake. "Your friend needs to be in the hospital for a few days, but since we can't arrange that, I'd suggest you get on that phone and find someplace for both of you. Without the proper attention, the arm could get infected. He could still die if you're not careful."

Dr. Rose walked to the stairway leading to his bedroom and turned. He took a long drink and stared at Judd. "You really think you know where my wife and baby are?"

Judd nodded.

Dr. Rose pointed to the mark on his forehead. "And because of this I'm not going?"

Judd pursed his lips and nodded again.

"I don't get it. I've tried to help people. You'd think God would take that into account."

"It's not about doing good things."

Before Judd could explain more, the doctor moved into the shadows. "I guess I had my chance." His voice cracked as he spoke again. "Do me a favor, would you?"

"If I can."

"Assuming you make it to where my wife and baby are, would you tell her I love her?"

The man's voice trailed off, and he whispered something Judd couldn't hear. It was clear he was in despair, and Judd wanted to say something to make him feel better, but what? What could he say to someone facing eternal separation from God and the people he loved?

Dr. Rose picked up the phone and dialed a number. "Judy, it's Pat. I'm taking a couple of days off. I really need to be away. Don't try my beeper or phone." He put the phone down, climbed the stairs, and Princess followed, whimpering. The door closed.

Judd grew tired. He found a pillow in the living room and carried it to the stairs leading to the basement.

The gunshot startled him. It came from Dr. Rose's bedroom. He dropped the pillow and took the stairs three at a time. Judd stopped at Dr. Rose's door and shook his head. He didn't look inside. He knew what he would find.

TEN

Running for Safety

LIONEL awoke with a headache and for the hundredth time reached for his forehead with the left hand that was no longer there. Several times during the day he reached to scratch his arm or pull it across his body, but he grabbed nothing but air.

He opened his eyes and tried to get used to the low light in their new hiding place. After moving Dr. Rose's body, Judd had used the man's computer to communicate with Chloe Steele. Chloe had found a safe house for them across the Ohio border where one of the members was a family doctor. The trip had been traumatic for Lionel. He had lost more blood, and some of the stitches had come out as Judd took back roads and cut across fields with the Humvee. But they had rendezvoused successfully with the new group, and the doctor had put Lionel on strict bed rest.

The safe house was dug into the earth at a historical site that had been all but forgotten by the Global Community. Most historical sites had been changed to somehow include Nicolae Carpathia and the Global Community. This one had been declared a disaster after the wrath of the Lamb earthquake, but the people there had fixed it up and used it to treat sick and desperate believers. The addition of the Humvee was welcomed, and Judd and Lionel felt good that the vehicle would be used for something positive.

Because of the way the safe house was situated, not many people came and went for fear of GC raids. And with what had happened in Indiana, the last thing Judd and Lionel wanted to do was be responsible for tipping the GC off.

Vicki had protested the decision, saying they could drive from Wisconsin and pick up Lionel and Judd, but even she had finally admitted that wasn't practical. Driving near any populated area, no matter what time of day, was dangerous for anyone without Carpathia's mark. Lionel felt bad they were still separated, and as the days wore on and his health improved, he longed to go north, not just to see Vicki, Mark, and the others, but also to find Zeke and see if the man could fit him with some kind of device for his missing arm.

Lionel not only regained his strength but also learned to function with only one hand. Eating wasn't a problem since Lionel could use one hand with most of the food. The doctor and everyone else in the new safe house had been amazed at what Lionel had done.

Their routine was much the same as other safe houses they had visited. During the day, people tried to sleep and stay quiet. At night, people used outdated computer connections to plan their next supply shipments with the Tribulation Force Co-op.

"When do you think we'll head north?" Lionel asked Judd a few weeks after they had arrived.

"I want you at 100 percent," Judd said. "It won't surprise me if this last leg of the trip is the hardest."

Vicki and the others in Wisconsin had rejoiced when they heard Lionel and Judd were safe, but Vicki despaired when she heard it would take a few weeks before Lionel could travel.

Cheryl had recovered from the birth of baby Ryan more quickly than Wanda expected. The woman had stayed an extra few days, helping Cheryl get used to feeding the baby and training the Fogartys on raising a child without doctor's visits.

Charlie had come up with the most surprising find of their stay. Months earlier, Marshall Jameson had discovered a GC warehouse on a routine Web search. From what Marshall could tell, the metal buildings held weapons and ammunition for GC forces in the Midwest. In a daring, nighttime raid, Charlie had accompanied Mark, Conrad, and the newest member of the team, Ty Spivey, to the facility, in spite of protests from Shelly, Tanya, and Vicki.

Instead of guns and bullet clips, they found medicine and food. Mark had deactivated the main alarm so the three strolled through the compound, taking much-needed pain relievers, cough medicine, and bandages.

Charlie had broken away from the other two and had found a tiny section of the building with baby formula, disposable diapers, and even shampoo. They brought all the supplies they could carry and made it back to the hideout before sunup.

Later, Tom Fogarty found information that the supplies had been confiscated by the GC and were supposed to be destroyed. *The GC wants everyone depending on them for everything,* Fogarty wrote the Trib Force. *Maybe some GC general or higher-up decided to put that stuff away in case it was ever needed. Maybe the guy was killed. I don't know, but I do know where the stuff in those buildings can get the best use.*

A week later a convoy of fearless Co-op drivers showed up with five semitrailers. One of the semis became buried in a sandy area near the buildings. Another reached a Trib Force storage center in Iowa and provided food and medicine for hundreds of families. But the three other trucks had been chased and apprehended by the GC. The drivers were beaten and questioned before being executed.

"No more of these missions until we know it's safe," Marshall Jameson said.

Vicki was even more depressed after the drivers' deaths. She had hoped to convince the others that Judd and Lionel needed to be in Wisconsin instead of Ohio. But with each day, a new report of GC activity seemed to block their return.

Vicki took comfort in the new life of Ryan Victor. The Fogartys were overjoyed with caring for the baby. The diapers Charlie had found were huge on the child, but Shelly rigged up a way to make them work. Everyone took turns holding him and helping Cheryl with anything she needed. It was almost like the boy had an unlimited set of brothers and sisters.

Vicki tried to stay current on the events around the world and especially news from Petra. Tsion Ben-Judah's letters continued to encourage people to stay strong as they passed the four-year mark of the Tribulation.

Sam Goldberg wrote more Petra Diaries, which made Vicki feel like she was in the ancient city. Sam's descriptions of Tsion Ben-Judah's messages, along with the testimonies of Micah and others, made her want to travel there. Sam described the battle going on for the soul of his new friend, and the kids prayed the boy would decide for God soon.

Sam Goldberg had tried everything to reach his new friend, Lev Taubman. Lev had moved with his family from Chicago to Jerusalem just before the disappearances, and they had spent the months before the escape to Petra hiding from the Global Community in secret passageways underneath the Holy City. Lev's father, mother, and older sister shared a small hut in Petra, and Sam had spent a lot of time talking with them.

They watched reports of miracles performed by devoted Carpathia followers, and Lev seemed moved by the dead raised to life and the people healed.

"You know what Dr. Ben-Judah says about them," Sam said.

"How could I not hear?" Lev said. "Fakers. Deceivers. They are not using the power of God, but the power of the evil one. Am I right?"

"Yes, but do you understand Tsion's message? These miracle workers were sent to draw you away from the true God to worship a false one."

Each day, as Tsion or Chaim followed the main teaching with an evangelistic message, Sam prayed for Lev and his family and the others who still had not believed in Christ. Each day he searched the foreheads of Lev's family for the mark of the believer, and each day Sam was disappointed.

Nothing could stop Sam from singing, praying, and celebrating with the people who had been turned around by the preaching and teaching. But Sam's heart ached when he thought of Lev and his family, who were so close to the truth.

Sam had found another new friend in Chang Wong, the teenager in New Babylon

Judd talked so much about. Chang had written Sam about one of his Petra Diaries, and the two had struck up a friendship. Sam asked Chang his opinion about unbelievers in Petra.

Chang wrote:

> Let me remind you that these people are just like you and me before the disappearances. There was a cloud over our understanding. You know this from Tsion's message. We are in a war for people's souls.
>
> Paul writes, "For we are not fighting against people made of flesh and blood, but against the evil rulers and authorities of the unseen world, against those mighty powers of darkness who rule this world, and against wicked spirits in the heavenly realms." There is something holding back your friend, and I will pray that God will break through before it's too late.
>
> My sister told me what happened to her in China recently. Three angels visited a group of unbelievers and preached the Good News to them. Some twenty-five of them received the mark of the believer before they were executed. God is at work. He is still calling people to follow him, so do not give up.

A few weeks later, Sam invited Lev to listen to Dr. Ben-Judah's teaching. That day, Tsion was to speak of the fruit of the Spirit from Galatians.

"I'll go with you if you'll go with me later," Lev said.

"Where?"

"Into the Negev. I hear a miracle worker is visiting us."

Sam frowned. "I have heard the rumors too."

"You don't believe he'll come?"

Sam shook his head. "I'm sure he will. Nicolae will try anything to get people to believe the lie that he is god—"

"I knew you would close your mind to this. My father said there was no sense inviting you."

"You and your family are in grave danger, and you don't understand it."

"My father read about the miracle workers in Mr. Williams's *The Truth*."

"And Mr. Williams made it clear every time he mentioned them that they are fakes. You can't trust them."

"My family will go, and we will at least hear them out. My father thinks they may give us a reprieve about the mark—"

"You're still considering taking Carpathia's mark? After all you've seen and heard here?"

Now it was Lev shaking his head. "You're so closed minded. You probably wouldn't even come to the debate they're talking about."

"What debate?"

"The one between your Dr. Ben-Judah and Leon Fortunato. Don't look at me that way. It's from a reliable person. They said it would be televised so the whole world could hear."

"I would welcome such a debate," Sam said. "Maybe you will finally see the truth."

"I still don't know who or what to believe, but getting out of this place for a couple of hours and walking into the desert to see a show, that interests me."

Sam thought of all he had seen God do while coming to Petra. People had been protected from bullets, missiles, and an army sent against them. What more did Lev need? Sam's lip trembled, and he looked away.

Lev grabbed his shoulder and turned him around. "Why are you crying?"

Sam stared. "I beg you not to go. You must convince your family not to follow the false messiahs. It could mean death to you."

Lev smiled. "I appreciate how much you care. I'll talk to my family."

Sam wandered back to camp, walking a different way than normal and praying, asking God to show him something new to speak to Lev. He spotted a man in his early thirties sitting by a campfire. Sam recognized him as a pilot friend of the American Rayford Steele. Sam walked closer, and the man motioned for him to sit.

"You look troubled, my young friend. My name is Abdullah."

Though he didn't know this man, Sam poured out Lev's story easily.

Abdullah listened and leaned forward when Sam finished. "I am not an outgoing person. Some would call me shy. But what you talk about has troubled me too. I have been pleading with those who are undecided, asking them not to go out. I've told them the only safety they can be assured of is here in Petra, and the only safety for their souls is in accepting the forgiveness of Jesus Christ."

"But what if they don't listen?" Sam said. "What if they go out anyway?"

Abdullah took a stick and traced it in the ashes surrounding the campfire. "There is only one way I know to make this piece of wood catch fire." He stuck it in the yellow blaze until the stick burned, then pulled it out. Flames licked at the wood and ran to the end. "The fire of God is ignited through the prayers of his people. I don't mean that God only acts on what we ask, but I have never seen a person come to God without prayer somehow being a part of it." Abdullah threw the stick into the flames. "How much have you prayed for your friend?"

"Every day."

"Good. Double that. Triple it. Pray every hour. I will add him to my list as well. Ask others to join you. Get on that e-mail thing the young people have—"

"The Young Trib Force?"

"Yes. Ask everyone to pray with lots of hardness."

"But what if nothing happens? What if we pray and Lev still goes out there?"

Abdullah stood. "When you are at war, you do not know how it will end. However, in this one, we know God wins, so we have the advantage. But we do not know what will happen in these battles for people's lives. Keep praying and asking God to work—pray that the eyes of Lev's heart will be opened. Pray that God will receive glory from Lev's life. And that he will finally understand the truth."

Abdullah's eyes twinkled in the firelight. "The results are not up to you. You can't make people believe. You must simply be faithful. If God brings someone to you, pray for them. Speak to them. Love them."

Sam watched the stick burn. "Why don't we pray right now?"

Abdullah smiled, clapped Sam's neck with a hand, and shook him gently. "Now you're talking with my language."

ELEVEN

The Hungry Earth

As Lionel improved over the next few weeks, Judd spent more time at the computer, reading *The Truth*, Sam's Petra Diaries, and anything else about the outside world. Judd was glad Lionel was making progress, but each time Judd saw him, he felt somehow betrayed, like Lionel had hurt himself to keep Judd away from Vicki. Of course, Judd knew this wasn't true, but something was going on inside him, a bitterness he knew had to be worked out.

Before the disappearances, Judd had felt this way about his parents. They were trying to hold him back, keep him from doing things, making his life hard.

Now Judd had a new perspective. His parents had tried to give him freedom and let him make his own decisions. At the time,

Judd figured they had no clue about his bad decisions, including turning his back on the church and God. But now Judd wondered if they *had* known. Had they sensed the battle inside him?

Thinking of his parents reminded Judd of the good times. When he was young, there was the excitement of summer, baseball, campouts, and vacation trips. Fall meant school, football, raking leaves, and preparing for the holidays. Winter was Christmas, snowball fights, skiing, and hockey. And spring meant baseball, heading outside, and planning for summer. The seasons had led from one to another in perfect sequence. It was part of the rhythm of life Judd took for granted.

But since the disappearances, those seasons had been interrupted. He used to be concerned about the weather and was bummed if it rained. Now he and the others stayed inside, scared to go out for fear of the Global Community. They did things at night, and Judd began to appreciate nocturnal animals and studied their living habits.

As the temperature turned colder, then plummeted severely, he resigned himself to staying in Ohio with their new friends. There was no way he and Lionel could set out on foot, and taking a vehicle was too dangerous. His trip north was on hold.

During this "underground season" as Judd called it, he looked forward to two things: writing or talking with Vicki and communicating with anyone else outside their group. Judd loved sending e-mails to Sam in Petra. He wrote Rayford Steele in San Diego and Chang Wong in New Babylon.

He also enjoyed writing Zeke in Wisconsin and hearing another perspective of things going on there. Zeke e-mailed texts of devotional messages by Marshall Jameson, and Judd was impressed by the tough issues he tackled. Marshall addressed becoming discouraged while being cooped up, fear of the Global Community, anger at God for making them go through the horrors of the Tribulation, and more. The one Judd was most interested in was a weeklong message Marshall had given on marriage. Several days were devoted to how husbands and wives were supposed to treat each other, but Marshall had begun by talking about whether it was good or bad to be focused on romantic relationships during such a terrible time.

The words challenged Judd to think more about Vicki, and they exchanged several e-mails about the material. What would a romance between Judd and Vicki do to their main purpose of spreading God's truth? Would it in any way take away from that goal, or would they be more effective together?

As Judd thought about the questions, an e-mail from Chang Wong in New Babylon arrived. *I wanted you to hear this for yourself,* Chang wrote. *I ran across it and think it shows the kind of evil we're up against.*

Judd opened the audio file and recognized the voices of Nicolae Carpathia and Leon Fortunato.

"If your wizards can do all these tricks, Leon, why can they not turn a whole sea back into salt water?"

"Excellency, that is a lot to ask. You must admit that they have done wonders for the Global Community."

"They have not done as much good as the Judah-ites have done bad, and that is the only scorecard that counts!"

"Your Worship, not to be contrary, but you are aware that Carpathian disciples all over the world have raised the dead, are you not?"

"I raised *myself* from the dead, Leon. These little tricks, bringing smelly corpses from graves just to amaze people and thrill the relatives, do not really compete with the Judah-ites', do they?"

"Turning wooden sticks into snakes? Impressive. Turning water to blood and then back again, then the water to wine? I thought you would particularly enjoy that one."

"I want converts, man! I want changed minds! When is your television debate with Ben-Judah?"

"Next week."

"And you are prepared?"

"Never more so, Highness."

"This man is clever, Leon."

"More than you, Risen One?"

"Well, of course not. But you must carry the ball. You must carry the day! And while you are at it, be sure to suggest to the cowardly sheep in Petra that an afternoon of miracles is planned, almost in their backyard, for later that same day."

"Sir, I had hoped we could test the area first."

"Test the area? Test the *area*?"

"Forgive me, Excellency, but where you have directed me to have a disciple stage that spectacle is so close to where we lost ground troops and weapons and where we have been unsuccessful in every attempt to interrupt their flying missions, not to mention where, my goodness, we dropped two bombs and a—"

"All right, I *know* what has gone on there, Leon! Who does not?! Test it if you must, but I want it convenient to those people. I want them filing out of that Siq and gathering for *our* event for a change. And when they see what my creature can do, we will start seeing wholesale moves from one camp to the other. You know who I want for that show, do you not?"

"Your best? I mean, one of your—"

"No less. Our goal should be to leave Petra a ghost town!"

"Oh, sir, I—"

"When did you become such a pessimist, Leon? We call you the Most High Reverend Father of Carpathianism, and I have offered myself as a living god, risen from the dead, with powers from on high. Yours is merely a sales job, Leon. Remind the people what their potentate has to offer, and watch them line up. And we have a special, you know."

"A special, sir?"

"Yes! We are running a special! This week only, anyone from Petra will be allowed to take the mark of loyalty with no punishment for having missed the deadline, now long since past. Think of the influence they can have on others just like them."

"The fear factor has worked fairly well, Potentate."

"Well, it *is* sort of a no-more-Mr.-Nice-Guy campaign, one would have to admit. But the time is past for worrying about my image. By now if people do not know who I am and what I am capable of, it is too late for them. But some blow to the other side, some victory over the curse of the bloody seas—that can only help. And I want you to do well against Ben-Judah, Leon. You are learned and devout, and you ask for worship of a living, breathing god who is here and who is not silent. It takes no faith to believe in the deity of one you can see on television every day. I should be the easy, convenient, logical choice."

"Of course, Majesty, and I shall portray you that way."

The conversation sent a chill down Judd's spine. Who was this creature Carpathia mentioned, and what would he do? Was there no end to Carpathia's evil? Judd prayed for Sam Goldberg and his friend who was not yet a believer. He asked God to help convince more people to turn to the true and living God.

There was excitement in Petra as Sam met with Abdullah to pray for Lev and his family. Sam found Abdullah singing near his tent, getting ready for the meeting that would beam Tsion's face via satellite to debate Leon Fortunato. Abdullah was hopeful that this would change many minds, but he was also excited about a flight he was making for the International Commodity Co-op.

"I think this trade we are about to make," Abdullah said, "is so big, only God could pull it off."

Sam smiled and the two began praying. Over the past few weeks, prayer had become more to Sam than simply telling God what he wanted. Sam was being drawn into something deeper, a reliance and trust in God that he couldn't explain. When Sam brought Lev, his family, and his other concerns to God, Sam felt God not only heard his requests but also took them like a weight from his shoulders. While Sam met with Lev later, he noticed he didn't feel as heavyhearted. He could simply talk naturally with his friend and show an interest in him.

The afternoon of the debate, Sam walked to Lev's home but couldn't find him. He asked a woman nearby where the Taubman family was, and she pointed and shook her head. "I don't know why the rabbi puts up with such people."

Sam climbed down to an area leading out of the city and spotted a gathering of thousands. Tsion Ben-Judah and Chaim

Rosenzweig were trying to quiet them. None of the people had the mark of the believer.

Sam noticed Lev's father and sister, who moved toward the front. "As soon as this debate is over, we're leaving here for a few hours to hear another speaker," Mr. Taubman said. "He will be right close by, and many believe he is the Christ. Jesus come back to earth to perform miracles and explain the future!"

Chaim stepped forward. "Please! You must not do this! Do you not know you are being deceived? You know of this only through the evil ruler of this world and his False Prophet. Stay here in safety. Put your trust in the Lord!"

Another man yelled something Sam couldn't hear. Then Tsion and Chaim continued pleading with the people. Chaim went so far as to say that these people were being used by the evil one to create chaos in the camp.

Lev's father raised a fist and pushed forward. "You take too much upon you. Why do you put yourselves above the congregation?"

Sam rushed into the crowd, keeping his eyes on Lev, who was with his mother in the middle of the throng. As he hurried forward, Tsion spoke. "The Lord knows who are his and who is holy. For what cause do you and all those gathered here speak against the Lord? And why would you murmur against Chaim?"

The shouting continued, and Sam reached Lev and caught his arm. "You have to come with me. You and your whole family."

"I can't leave now," Lev said. "Listen, my father is speaking."

"We will not stand with you," Lev's father said. "Is it a small thing that you have taken us from our motherland, our homes where we had plenty, and brought us to this rocky place where all we have to eat is bread and water, and you set yourself up as a prince over us?"

Sam couldn't believe what he was hearing. It was just like the children of Israel in the Old Testament, crying out to Moses in the wilderness. Sam sensed something terrible was about to happen, but he couldn't leave his friend. He pleaded with Lev and Mrs. Taubman. "Come with me to the rocky place where you can see better."

Lev and his mother hesitated, then followed.

Sam glanced at Tsion Ben-Judah. The words of Lev's father and the others seemed to wound the man so much that he cried out to God. "Lord, forgive them, for they know not what they do. I have neither set myself over them nor demanded anything from them except respect for you."

Sam pulled Lev and his mother onto a ledge just as Tsion looked over the crowd and said, "God is telling Chaim and me to separate ourselves from you to save ourselves from his wrath."

People shouted at Tsion and Chaim. Many fell on their faces and cried out. Some stood and shook their fists. Sam couldn't hear their words, but he had a sick feeling.

Lev yelled for his father. The man glanced at the boy, shook his head, and glared. His sister screamed angrily at Tsion. Lev took a step toward his father, but Sam stopped him.

Tsion quieted the crowd and spoke gravely. "Unless you agree with these, it would do well for you to depart from the presence of these wicked men, lest you be consumed in all their sins. From this point on, let it be known that the Lord has sent me to do all these works; I do not do them in my own interest. If these men do what is in their minds to do and God visits a plague of death on them, then all shall understand that these men have provoked the Lord."

When Tsion finished, the rocks trembled. Lev and his mother fell back, and Sam grabbed them as a great hole opened under hundreds of people. The angry men and women were swallowed immediately, falling into a deep cavern. Lev's father and sister screamed and plunged down, their arms waving as they fell. The wails echoed from the enormous hole, and just as suddenly as the earth had opened, it closed, and the people inside disappeared.

Thousands scattered, screaming as they ran. Lev shook with fear and his mother yelled, "Get out, before we're killed too!"

Before Sam could stop them, the two had crawled over another ledge and ran for their home. Tsion and Chaim prayed together at the front.

Sam looked back again and watched Lev keep his mother from falling. "Please, God, I pray you won't let their hearts be hardened by this. Lev and Mrs. Taubman still have a chance to believe your truth. Help Tsion as he debates Leon Fortunato. May something he says stir their hearts. And help me to reach out before it is too late."

TWELVE

The Great Debate

SAM climbed over the ledge as thousands scattered from the area. The image of people plunging to their deaths stuck with him. He heard Lev's mother weeping when he approached their small home, so he sat outside the door and prayed for them.

A half hour later, the door opened and Lev stepped outside and sat next to Sam. The two were silent for some time.

Then Lev looked at Sam with tears in his eyes. "Why would God do that to my father and sister?"

"I'm so sorry for your loss," Sam said, his chin quivering.

"I was just thinking about the miracle workers," Lev said. "If my father's and sister's bodies were here, we could take them to the miracle workers and they could be raised. I've seen that happen on the reports."

Sam shook his head. "Those people cannot offer you or anyone else real life. They are fakes. They want you to worship Nicolae."

"I don't care. I want my father back."

Sam closed his eyes and thought of his own father. "I know what it's like to lose a dad. It's painful, but your father's choice doesn't have to be yours. Do not harden your heart toward the one who loves you."

"How can God love me if he takes away my father?"

"Your father spoke out against God's leaders. God is cutting out those who don't believe. You must follow him before it is too late."

Lev shook his head. "I have to help my mother. She is all I have now."

"Please, listen to the debate. Tsion will explain things."

"I'll try to listen," Lev said.

After Lev had gone back inside, Sam lingered a few moments, praying for him. He ran to find Mr. Stein but was stopped short by the voice of Tsion Ben-Judah. Sam climbed back over a ridge and saw Tsion in front of a crowd. A camera stood before him.

"I would ask that all pray during the broadcast that the Lord give me his wisdom and his words. And as for you who still plan to venture away from this safe place, let me plead with you one more time not to do it, not to make yourself vulnerable to the evil one. Let the Global Community and their Antichrist and his False Prophet make ridiculous claims about fake miracle workers. Do not fall into their trap.

"Messiah himself warned his disciples of this very thing. He told them, 'Many false prophets shall rise, and shall deceive many. And because iniquity shall abound, the love of many shall wax cold. But he who endures to the end, he shall be saved. And this gospel of the kingdom shall be preached in all the world for a witness unto all nations.' "

Sam glanced at the huge screen above the stage. Was Tsion being carried over GCNN live?

" 'If any man says to you, "Lo, here is Christ," believe it not,' " Tsion continued. " 'For there shall arise false Christs and false prophets, and they shall show great signs and wonders—so much so that if it were possible, they would deceive even you. If they say to you, "Behold, he is in the desert," do not go.

"Behold, he is in the secret chambers,"
believe it not.' "

※

Judd and the others in the Ohio hideout
huddled together to stay warm and kept the
television sound low. One of the leaders led
in prayer that God would give Tsion success
and boldness.

Something was wrong at the Global
Community News Network. Tsion was
already on the air and warning people not to
follow the false Christs. A woman from New
Babylon appeared on-screen and asked Dr.
Ben-Judah to stand by to speak with the Most
High Reverend Father Fortunato.

"Thank you, ma'am, but rather than stand
by, as you flip your switches and do whatever
it is you have to do to make this work, let me
begin by saying that I do not recognize Mr.
Fortunato as most high anything, let alone
reverend or father."

The screen split and Leon Fortunato
appeared in one of his colorful outfits. A few
people in the hideout snickered, and Judd
closed his eyes. He would give anything to be
back with his friends in Wisconsin, listening
to their comments about Leon's clothes.

"Greetings, Dr. Ben-Judah, my esteemed

opponent. I heard some of that and may I say I regret that you have characteristically chosen to begin what has been intended as a cordial debate with a vicious character attack. I shall not lower myself to this and wish only to pass along my welcome and best wishes."

Tsion didn't say anything, and Judd wondered if he could hear. Finally, the rabbi said, "Is it my turn, then? Shall I open by stating the case for Jesus as the Christ, the Messiah, the Son of the living—"

The woman broke into the conversation and tried to avoid the conflict. After a few moments of banter, Leon Fortunato began. Judd thought the man looked more composed, even gentle, as he started his remarks. "My premise is simple. I proclaim Nicolae Carpathia, risen from the dead, as the one true god, worthy of worship, and the savior of mankind. He is the one who surfaced at the time of the greatest calamity in the history of the world and has pulled together the global community in peace and harmony and love. You claim Jesus of Nazareth as both the Son of God and one with God, which makes no sense and cannot be proven. This leaves you and your followers worshiping a man who was no doubt very spiritual, very bright, perhaps enlightened, but who is now dead. If he were alive and as all-powerful as you say, I challenge him to strike me dead where I sit."

"I don't believe this," Lionel whispered. "I wish God would strike him right now."

But nothing happened. Leon smiled, cocked his head, and said, "Hail Carpathia, our lord and risen king."

Tsion Ben-Judah jumped into the debate. "I trust you will spare us the rest of the hymn written by and about the egomaniac who murders those who disagree with him. I raise up Jesus the Christ, the Messiah, fully God and fully man, born of a virgin, the perfect lamb who was worthy to be slain for the sins of the whole world. If he is but a man, his sacrificial death was only human and we who believe in him would be lost.

"But Scripture proves him to be all that he claimed to be. His birth was foretold hundreds, yea, thousands of years before it was fulfilled in every minute detail. He himself fulfills at least 109 separate and distinct prophecies that prove he is the Messiah."

Judd's heart welled up, and tears stung his eyes. Tsion's message was as rapid-fire as a machine gun, and Judd was thrilled that people around the world could hear it.

"The uniqueness and genius of Christianity," Tsion continued, "is that the Virgin Birth allowed for the only begotten Son of God to identify with human beings without surrendering his godly, holy nature. Thus he could die for the sins of the whole world. His Father's resurrecting him from the dead three days later proves that God was satisfied with his sacrifice for our sins.

"Not only that, but I have discovered, in my exhaustive study of the Scriptures, more than 170 prophecies by Jesus himself in the four Gospels alone. Many have already been literally fulfilled, guaranteeing that those that relate to still future events will also be literally fulfilled. Only God himself could write history in advance—incredible evidence of the deity of Jesus Christ and the supernatural nature of God."

Leon stared into the camera. Judd wondered if Nicolae himself was watching this spectacle, and if so, how red Carpathia's face must be.

"But we *know* our king and potentate arose from the dead," Fortunato said, "because we saw it with our own eyes. If there is one anywhere on this earth who saw Jesus resurrected, let him speak now or forever hold his peace. Where is he? Where is this Son of God, this man of miracles, this king, this

Savior of mankind? If your Jesus is who you say he is, why are you hiding in the desert and living on bread and water?

"The god of this world lives in a palace and provides good gifts to all those who worship him."

"Mr. Fortunato," Tsion calmly said, "would you tell the viewers how many people have died by the guillotine because of your loving god? Would you admit that Global Community troops and equipment were swallowed by the earth near Petra, and that two bombs and a deadly missile struck here, yet no one has been injured and no structure jeopardized? Will you not also admit that Global Community Security and Intelligence Peacekeeping forces have spent millions of Nicks on attacking all traffic in and out of this place, and not one plane, flier, or volunteer has been scratched?"

Leon ignored Tsion's questions and praised Carpathia for his worldwide rebuilding effort. "Those who die by the blade choose this for themselves. Nicolae is not willing that any should perish but that all should be loyal and committed to him."

"But, sir, the population has been cut to half what it once was, the seas are dead from the curse of blood—prophesied in the Bible and sent by God. Yet the believers—his children, at least the ones who have survived the

The Great Debate

murderous persecution of the man you
would enthrone as god—are provided water
and food from heaven, not just here, but in
many areas around the world."

Leon praised Nicolae as a man of peace
and accused Ben-Judah followers of being
the problem. At one point he criticized Tsion
as one of the "disloyal Jews."

"Mr. Fortunato, I wear the title as a badge
of honor. I am humbled beyond measure to
be one of God's chosen people. Indeed, the
entire Bible is testament to his plan for us for
the ages, and it is being played out for the
whole world to see even as we speak."

Fortunato smiled. "But are you not the
ones who killed Jesus?"

"On the contrary," Tsion said. "Jesus himself
was a Jew, as you well know. And the fact is
that the actual killing of Christ was at the
hands of Gentiles. He stood before a Gentile
judge, and Gentile soldiers put him on the
cross.

"Oh, there was an offense against him on
the part of Israel that the nation and her people must bear. In the Old Testament book of
Zechariah, chapter 12, verse 10 prophesies that
God will 'pour upon the house of David, and
upon the inhabitants of Jerusalem, the spirit of
grace and of supplications; and they shall look

unto me whom they have pierced, and they shall mourn for him.'

"Israel must confess a specific national sin against the Messiah before we will be blessed. In Hosea 5:15, God says he will 'go and return to my place, till they acknowledge their offense, and seek my face; in their affliction they will seek me earnestly.'

"The offense? Rejecting the messiahship of Jesus. We repent of that by pleading for his return. He will come yet again and set up his earthly kingdom, and not only I but also the Word of God itself predicts the doom of the evil ruler of this world when that kingdom is established."

"Well," Leon said, "thank you for that fascinating history lesson. But I rejoice that *my* lord and king is alive and well, and I see him and speak with him every day. Thank you for being a quick and worthy opponent."

Judd shook his head. "Fortunato never answered any of Tsion's arguments."

"What did you expect?" Lionel said.

Sam was mesmerized by the interaction between Tsion and Fortunato. Hundreds of thousands of supporters gathered, many with heads bowed in prayer.

Leon looked into the camera and tilted his head, as if he were talking to the crowd. "I would like to greet the many citizens of the Global Community who reside with you temporarily," he said, "and invite them to enjoy the benefits and privileges of the outside world. I trust many will join one of our prophets and teachers and workers of miracles when he ministers in your area less than an hour from now. He will—"

Tsion interrupted, "The Scriptures tell us that many deceivers are entered into the world, who confess not that Jesus Christ is come in the flesh. Such a one is a deceiver and an antichrist."

"If you'll allow me to finish, sir—"

"Whoever abides not in the doctrine of Christ, has not God. He who abides in the doctrine of Christ, he has both the Father and the Son. If any come to you and bring not this doctrine, do not receive him into your house, neither bid him Godspeed, for he who bids Godspeed partakes of his evil deeds."

"All right then, you've worked in all your tiresome Bible verses. I shall be content to merely thank you and—"

"For as long as you have me on international television, Mr. Fortunato, I feel obligated to preach the gospel of Christ and to speak forth the words of Scripture. The Bible says the Word shall not return void, and so I would like to quote—"

The screen went blank as the Global Community finally cut Tsion off. A cheer rose from the crowd for Tsion, and Sam noticed Lev Taubman a few feet behind him.

"How long have you been here?" Sam said.

"I saw most of it."

Lev looked tired or scared. Sam couldn't tell which. Suddenly, a group of people shaking their fists at Tsion moved toward the Siq to go outside Petra. Others screamed warnings, but the people wouldn't listen.

"Are you leaving with them?" Sam said to Lev.

Before Lev could respond, Tsion cried out over the noise, " 'Be sober, be vigilant; because your adversary the devil walks about like a roaring lion, seeking whom he may devour.' "

Sam watched the people walk toward the desert. He had heard the GC had constructed a stage almost two miles from the entrance to Petra.

Lev turned. "The Global Community is offering forgiveness for not taking the mark, even though the deadline is long passed. It's tempting."

"And what do you think?"

Lev ran a hand through his hair. "I need to stay with my mother."

Sam took the boy by his shoulders. "Lev, I have been praying for you nonstop. God wants you to come to him. He wants you to choose life."

"I am thankful that you care, and after what happened to my father and sister, believe me, I have more questions, but—"

"Let me help you answer them. What is keeping you from believing in Jesus as your Messiah?"

Lev shook his head. "I don't know. I'm confused. What Dr. Ben-Judah said makes sense. . . ." He licked his lips. "Let's go up to the high place. I have a pair of strong binoculars. If this is a trick by the GC, I will do as you say."

"Don't put the decision off," Sam said, but Lev was gone, running toward his house for the binoculars.

THIRTEEN

Valley of Death, Prayer of Life

SAM climbed with Lev up to the high place and looked out over the desert. The concert stage had been set up quickly, and people moved in a long line toward it. As an airplane landed on the runway nearby, a helicopter flew out to meet it.

"One of the reasons it makes no sense to go out there is the protection we have here," Sam said, handing the binoculars to Lev. "The helicopter pilot is my friend Abdullah Smith. He says the GC tries to shoot our planes and helicopters down, but it is no use. God is protecting us."

Several hundred people walked through the hot sand toward the venue. Lev clicked the binoculars to increase the power and punched Sam in the shoulder. "Looks like your friends in the chopper are going to the show as well."

Sam grabbed the glasses and looked closely. Sure enough, Abdullah's chopper flew toward the stage. Sam watched the reaction of armed Peacekeepers as the chopper sat down a hundred feet from the stage, whipping up a sandy cloud. There was a brief standoff, with the chopper starting up again, and then the GC left the craft alone.

While the crowd made its way to the stage, Sam continued explaining the Scriptures about Jesus. It was the same message Lev had heard from Chaim and Tsion for many weeks, but Sam thought that perhaps this time the words would sink in and the boy's heart would soften.

When the people were in place, someone onstage captured their attention. Sam and Lev couldn't see the stage, but they could tell from the crowd reaction that the people were impressed.

Suddenly the crowd looked up, shading their eyes from the sun. A white cloud appeared over the gathering and blocked the hot rays.

"What do you make of that?" Lev said.

Sam kept his eyes on the people. The cloud disappeared, and moments later a spring of water gushed from the middle of the group, and people drank from it.

Lev took the binoculars. "They're passing around a basket of food."

Sam shook his head. "I see what's happening. Whoever is up there is trying to prove he can do God's miracles. Lev, you need to pray—"

"A hundred people just fell to the ground! It looks like they're dead!"

Sam took the binoculars and viewed the chaos. People shrieked, some turned and ran, and then everyone froze.

"Look there," Lev said, pointing to a small cloud of dust rolling like a tumbleweed toward the gathering. "What could that be?"

Sam glanced at the cloud and shook his head, focusing on the group again. "I don't know, but the people look deathly afraid of it."

Suddenly the spring turned to blood. People backed away, then fled toward Petra. Many screamed and staggered in the sand, trying desperately to retreat.

"The dust cloud just changed direction," Lev said. "It's headed for all those people. Could that be some kind of animal?"

The chopper started, and a cloud of dust kicked up and covered the area. Sam strained to see through the binoculars. When the sand cleared, Lev let out a shriek. Bodies dotted the path back to Petra. The stage was gone. There were no Peacekeepers or vehicles or anything that had been there only moments ago.

Sam, his hands shaking, gave the binoculars to Lev, but the boy was on his knees, tears streaming from his face. "That could have been me out there. If I had gone, I would be dead right now."

Sam knelt beside him. "Take this last chance to turn to God and away from the enemy of your soul. Nicolae and his followers would like you to curse the true God and take Nicolae's mark, but God—"

"I'm ready," Lev interrupted. "And not just because I'm afraid. I do believe what you've said about Jesus. I opened the Scriptures and read the passages Tsion has given. I don't know why I haven't seen it before, but I'm ready to pray."

Sam put a hand on the boy's shoulder and prayed. Lev repeated Sam's words softly. "Heavenly Father, thank you for sending your Son, Jesus, to pay the penalty for my sin. I believe that he died in my place, and right now I ask you to forgive me of my sin. I'm sorry I've rejected you and the gift you've offered, but now I reach out and take it by faith. And because Jesus rose from the dead, I know you have prepared the way for me to spend eternity with you. Thank you for saving me from death today, for saving my soul, and I ask you to come into my life and lead me and show me your path for the rest of my days. In Jesus' name. Amen."

When Lev looked up, Sam saw the mark of the believer on his forehead. Lev wiped tears from his eyes and stood. "Let's go talk with my mother."

※

Vicki couldn't wait until midnight each night. That was the time she and Judd agreed to communicate with each other. They limited themselves to three times a week talking by phone, and the other nights they used the computer.

In one e-mail, Judd described his thoughts about Lionel. *I feel awful that I resent him. I know there's no part of him that wanted that to happen, and he's been through so much pain during the healing process. Yesterday I awoke out of a dead sleep and heard him gasping for breath. I thought he was dying, Vick, but when I got to him, he was crying. He said his arm really hurt, and he was just sad about the things he'd never be able to do again.*

All that must make it even harder for you, Vicki wrote.

Yeah. Deep down I know that what happened

is not anybody's fault. But when I think of not being able to be there with you, all those ugly feelings come back.

Vicki had slept on it and had brought up the subject the next night on the phone. "I've been thinking more about you and Lionel." She paused. Over time she and Judd had been able to share some deep things without holding back.

"God protected you and Lionel from the GC," Vicki continued. "Even though the others in that group were killed, he spared you two for a reason. I don't know why we've had to be apart so long, and my heart aches just as much as yours about the separation, but one of the good things for me has been that I know we don't have to be together in order to show love to each other. I'd hate to think of this happening, but if we never saw each other again before the return of Jesus, that would be okay. If God wants us together, I know we will be. If he just wants us to be friends and help each other along the next few years, then that's okay too."

"Totally surrendered," Judd muttered.

"What?"

"I was just thinking about being surrendered to God. Letting him control things and resting in his love for us takes a lot of the pressure off. I can't imagine not seeing you, but you're right. If God wants us to stay apart, I can handle it. But I don't think he wants that, do you?"

"I hope not," Vicki said quickly, then laughed.

"When you look at things that way, with God in control, there's no way I can blame Lionel for us not being together."

"Tell Lionel Zeke is working on a gadget he thinks Lionel will be able to use. I hope we'll be able to see him soon too."

Vicki and Judd always ended their conversations and e-mails with prayer. Sometimes one would pray, sometimes both. Most of their talks lasted hours, and several times the sun had come up before they finished.

The Wisconsin group had a routine of eating the morning meal together, then having a time of teaching and prayer. It was Vicki's turn to give a brief devotional one morning, and she happened to see the latest Petra Diary from Sam. She brought a printed copy to the meeting and gave everyone the good news that the boy they had prayed for, Lev Taubman, and his mother had become believers.

"Let me read the latest entry that proves we don't wrestle against flesh and blood, but against a spiritual enemy. Sam writes, 'Lev and I saw something incredible happen in the desert, but it wasn't until I spoke with my friend Abdullah that I found out what really happened. Abdullah was in the desert when people from Petra ventured out to see the miracle worker.

" 'Abdullah said the man looked like a younger version of Leon Fortunato, and the man said he was not from this world and that he had been given power by the risen lord, Nicolae Carpathia.

" 'The first miracle the guy did was bring in a cloud that blocked the sun. Then the guy made the cloud disappear, not move or fall apart, but vanish. Next he turned the microphone and stand into a giant snake. Everybody recoiled, but just as fast as he turned it into a snake, it was a microphone and stand again.

" 'Then from the middle of the crowd came a spring of water gushing straight into the air. People drank from it. The man asked if people were hungry and produced a basket of real bread, warm and chewy. Everyone in the crowd took some, but the basket never emptied.

" 'Do you see the mockery of this? Miracles God performed in the Bible were produced by this faker to gain people's trust. And they fell for it big-time. The man, or being, whatever he was, said he was a disciple of Carpathia. And while his behavior had been nice up to that point, he then said that Carpathia's patience had run out and that he would administer Carpathia's mark. He simply pointed at people, and they had the mark of Nicolae.

" 'This is where the story really gets ugly. The man killed more than a hundred at one time. People went crazy. Then the man raised the dead people back to life. It went on like that, the man convincing people their friends were really dead. Then a little cloud of dust appeared on the horizon.

" 'I have to tell you, Lev and I saw this cloud moving straight for the stage and audience, but we didn't know what it was. Abdullah said the man onstage told the people the cloud contained snakes, vipers with a deadly venom. That's when the spring of water turned to blood and the man called the people fools and said Nicolae wanted them dead. He told them to run but warned that the vipers would kill them before they reached Petra.

" 'And that is what happened. The cloud caught up to the people, and there was a line of bodies in the sand. Abdullah was sitting in the helicopter with two of his friends when the evil man appeared before them. The wonder-worker didn't open his mouth, but they heard him say, "I know who you are. I know you by name. Your god is weak and your faith a sham, and your time is limited. You shall surely die." ' "

Vicki glanced at the group and saw looks of disbelief. Shelly and Janie shook from the horrific story.

Charlie looked up with glassy eyes. "Didn't any of them survive?"

"All of the people on foot died. Abdullah and the others in the chopper were okay because they were believers. Sam wrote that when the dust settled, everything on the desert—the stage, the vehicles, the Peace-keepers—was gone."

"It was all an illusion?" Tanya said.

Vicki folded the paper. "I don't know what it was. Tsion told Abdullah and some others that the man was probably a demonic appa-rition."

"A what?" Charlie said.

"A demon in human form. Tsion referred to Revelation 12 that says that when Satan was cast out of heaven the other bad angels were cast out with him. John 10:10 says Satan wants only to steal and to kill and to destroy. So it all fits.

"Take heart in this," Vicki concluded. "I'll read you the last part of Sam's letter.

" 'Dr. Ben-Judah told his friends that God is doing his "winnowing work." This means he is cleaning the earth of his enemies, wiping them out, and allowing those who still haven't chosen for God to face the consequences. Dr. Ben-Judah concluded with a verse from Romans. "O the depth of the riches both of the wisdom and knowledge of God! How unsearchable are his judgments, and his ways past finding out! For who hath known the mind of the Lord? Or who hath been his counselor? . . . For of him, and through him, and to him, are all things—to whom be glory for ever." '

"Sam finishes with this. 'We need to be careful about the deception of the evil one, but the good news is that there are still more people to reach. May God give each of us new opportunities, even today, to come in contact with the undecided and convince them that God loves them.' "

Sam met with Lev and his mother early the next morning in Petra. The two admitted they had never read much of the Bible. As they munched their morning manna, Sam helped them understand an overview of the Scriptures.

A buzz spread through the million-member camp that everyone should gather after breakfast. Sam took a break from teaching, and the three went to the meeting place. Mrs. Taubman's heart was heavy about losing her daughter and husband, and Sam could tell Lev was struggling too. He tried to comfort them as much as he could before Chaim Rosenzweig, known as Micah, spoke.

"Tsion believes the Lord has told him that no more indecision reigns in the camp. You may confirm that by looking about you. Is there anyone in this place without the mark of the believer? Anyone anywhere? We will not pressure or condemn you. This is just for our information."

Sam looked around at the people near him. Everyone he saw had the mark of the believer.

After a few minutes, Tsion Ben-Judah stepped forward. "The prophet Isaiah predicted that 'it shall come to pass in that day that the remnant of Israel, and such as have escaped of the house of Jacob, will never again depend on him who defeated them, but will depend on the Lord, the Holy One of Israel, in truth.

" 'The remnant will return, the remnant of Jacob, to the Mighty God. For though your people, O Israel, be as the sand of the sea, a remnant of them will return. . . .' And of the evil ruler of this world who has tormented you, Isaiah says further, 'It shall come to pass in that day that his burden will be taken away from your shoulder, and his yoke from your neck, and the yoke will be destroyed.' Praise the God of Abraham, Isaac, and Jacob.

"The prophet Zechariah quoted our Lord God himself, speaking of the land of Israel, that 'two-thirds of it shall be cut off and die, but one-third shall be left in it. I will bring the one-third through the fire, will refine them as silver is refined, and test them as gold is tested. They will call on My name and I will answer them. I will say, "This is My people." And each one will say, "The Lord is my God." '

"My dear friends, you remnant of Israel, this is in accord with the clear teaching of Ezekiel, chapter 37, where our barren nation is seen in the last days to be a valley of dry bones, referred to by the Lord himself as 'the whole house of Israel. They indeed say, "Our bones are dry, our hope is lost, and we ourselves are cut off!" '

"But then, dear ones, God said to Ezekiel, 'Therefore prophesy and say to them, "Thus says the Lord God: 'Behold, O My people, I will open your graves and cause you to come up from your graves, and bring you into the land of Israel. . . . I will put My Spirit in you, and you shall live, and I will place you in your own land. Then you shall know that I, the Lord, have spoken it and performed it.' "' "

Sam looked at Lev and his mother. Sam was grateful he had been part of God's rescue plan for them both.

FOURTEEN

Blood in the Water

JUDD sat in the early morning darkness, staring at an old map of the United States of America. It had been months since he and Lionel had arrived at the Ohio safe house, and things had changed drastically. An all-out blitz on believers from the Global Community had left few safe places between this location and Wisconsin. Commander Kruno Fulcire appeared daily, rewarding loyal citizens for finding hidden believers.

Judd had even recognized two who were beheaded shortly after they appeared on live broadcasts. Fulcire seethed at those who avoided taking Carpathia's mark. Citizens hunted down the unmarked for cash to help keep themselves alive. Many were hungry, and it became more and more difficult to move supplies.

The food situation for the Ohio safe house had become bleak. They didn't have manna from heaven or quail that flew in for dinner every day like Petra. With an influx of new people, the once huge hiding place got smaller. Judd no longer ruled the computer, and it became difficult to keep his appointments with Vicki.

The doctor who had helped Lionel at the safe house moved with a few others to another location Judd had helped build. The work had been done only at night, and though there were several scares, the GC hadn't discovered their secret operation.

Lionel had been depressed that he couldn't help with the digging and physical work, but he had kept in contact with other Trib Force locations and with Chloe Steele. She had tried to get supplies from the Co-op to their location, but it was difficult with all the GC activity. Lionel had catalogued their supply list and put everyone on a ration system.

Despite the negatives, Judd knew God was still working. Another plague had hit the earth, turning rivers into rushing floods of blood. Judd had traveled past a nearby river every night on his way to the construction area, and the gurgling blood and horrible smell was sickening. One night he had stood in the moonlight, looking at a river so dark it seemed like a bottomless pit. He had found it difficult to sleep, having nightmares about blood washing over him, and that was the last time he walked close to the river.

The bloody water caused people to focus less on hunting down people without Carpathia's mark and more on staying alive, which had been good for believers. People were still coming to the truth and giving their lives to God through the kids' Web site, which Judd had all but abandoned with the construction project. Lionel kept Judd up-to-date with new contacts and anything he learned.

Reports from around the world came in about sightings of angels preaching in remote areas. Lionel nearly attacked Judd early one morning as he came in, muddy and sweating from a night of work.

"You've got to see this," Lionel said, pulling Judd toward the computer.

Judd stared at the message from Chang.

I just heard a story from our Co-op group in Argentina. Rayford Steele is one of the pilots. Rayford and some others found themselves in a group of locals moving through the countryside. They finally found someone who spoke English and asked where everyone was going.

The people said they had been invited by three men who came to their door and told them to meet together to hear good news. They told them not to be afraid, even though none of these people had the mark of Carpathia. Pretty soon, the GC showed up, about a hundred troops.

Judd felt goose bumps as he read. He wiped a finger clean, pressed the computer's down arrow, and read the rest of the message.

The GC told them they couldn't meet together and that they had twenty-four hours to take the mark of Carpathia or face death. But the people didn't pay attention. Then, as the man on the bullhorn shouted his final warning, someone called for silence.

"One of the angels," Judd said under his breath as he scrolled down.

It was the angel Christopher. He intro-duced his coworkers, Nahum and Caleb, and then ordered the GC troops to leave the area or face death by God's hand. They did leave, and after that the angels repeated the message we have heard about all around the world.

Judd secretly wished he would be visited by some kind of angel that could pick him up and drop him in Wisconsin. He had seen angelic visitors on television and had heard about them from Vicki and others, but he had never seen or spoken with one in person.

Now, as he sat looking at the map and estimating the number of miles between him and Vicki, he ran his finger along the waterways. Many of them had changed since the great earthquake, but he wondered if he had some kind of boat that would float in the blood. . . .

Judd put his head on the map and closed his eyes. There was word of a Global Community stronghold being built south of the bombed-out city of Chicago. If that was true, Judd knew it would take a miracle to get to Wisconsin.

Judd thought of the verses he had looked up about patience and perseverance. The Bible spoke in various ways about hanging in during the tough times, and Judd had written every reference down and had committed several to memory.

His favorite was from Romans, and Judd softly mouthed the words. " 'We can rejoice, too, when we run into problems and trials, for we know that they are good for us—they help us learn to endure. And endurance develops strength of character in us, and character strengthens our confident expectation of salvation. And this expectation will not disappoint us.' "

I don't want any more character, God, Judd thought. *I just want to get back to Vicki.*

Vicki and the others in Wisconsin made the most of every opportunity given to them to tell people about God. Their main contact with the outside world was through the Internet, and everyone rejoiced when a new person came to Christ. Janie had made red hearts out of some old fabric she had found. Each time they received word of a person receiving the mark of the believer, she put a heart on the wall above the computer. "Another heart snatched from that evil Nicolae," she said.

Jim Dekker, the computer whiz who had worked for the Global Community before coming to live with the kids, had developed another version of The Cube, the high-tech presentation of the gospel. Though hackers loyal to the GC had tried to corrupt the files, Jim had defeated their attempts.

The Fogartys, Tom and Josey, had taken to baby Ryan as soon as he had been born. A few months after his birth, the baby went on formula Charlie and the others had found. Unlike the situation in Ohio, Vicki's group had plenty to eat and a supply that would last months and perhaps years.

As the baby grew, Vicki noticed a sadness in Cheryl. When the Fogartys were with the baby in the main cabin, she avoided them. Cheryl skipped many of their devotion times, saying she needed more sleep or wasn't feeling well. Every time Vicki tried to talk with her about it, Cheryl changed the subject. By the time Ryan started to crawl, Cheryl had moved into a run-down shack by herself farthest away from the others. At each milestone in the baby's life—his first tooth, his first haircut, his first word, which was *dada*—Cheryl withdrew more and more.

Though Cheryl's attitude concerned Vicki, there was still much to be excited about. Tanya and Ty Spivey, along with the other believers who had broken away from the cult in the cave, grew in their faith almost as quickly as Ryan gained weight. They were at every meeting, every prayer vigil, and were some of the first to read Tsion Ben-Judah's Web site and Sam Goldberg's Petra Diaries.

Vicki had become resigned to Judd's absence. She knew how dangerous it was to travel, and though there were nights when she wanted to jump into Marshall Jameson's van and barrel south, she knew it was best to wait.

Her love for Judd grew, even as their talks via computer and phone became less frequent. Both Judd and Vicki had been asked to cut down their time, so Vicki wrote her thoughts and prayers and typed them when others weren't around.

The older women had been a big help to Vicki, especially Josey Fogarty, who counseled her and gave advice when Vicki felt alone. Vicki would hold baby Ryan as he slept, listening to Josey. The woman had spent years waiting on her husband to become a believer, so she had developed a lot of patience.

The most surprising person to help her was Zeke. She figured he wouldn't understand, but Zeke had listened and even gave Vicki a verse to memorize from James. On top of the page, Zeke had scrawled a note. *When you get down and don't think you can go on, look at this. It's almost like God put this in his Word especially for you, though it's helped me a lot since my dad died. Remember, God has a plan, and he's going to do something special with you and Judd.*

The verses came from the first chapter of

James. Vicki memorized them, and God brought the words to mind at crucial times. *"Dear brothers and sisters, whenever trouble comes your way, let it be an opportunity for joy. For when your faith is tested, your endurance has a chance to grow. So let it grow, for when your endurance is fully developed, you will be strong in character and ready for anything."*

"What are you preparing me for?" Vicki prayed. "I'm not sure I want whatever it is. But, God, I trust you. Everything in me trusts you. Please provide some way for us to get back together."

A few days before Ryan's eight-month birthday, which Vicki and the others celebrated with gusto, a vehicle pulled into camp. Zeke had helped many believers take on new identities with false papers and even false marks, but as the GC stepped up their efforts to kill anyone without the mark, Zeke's work tailed off. There was almost no one who needed uniforms to tailor or disguises to invent.

When Marshall Jameson opened the door, Vicki gasped. It was Chad Harris, a friend from Iowa who had taken Vicki and the others in after they had escaped a GC facility. Chad had helped Vicki get through the death of her friend Pete.

Chad shook hands with everyone and smiled at Vicki. "Zeke told me you were here, but I didn't believe I'd ever see you again."

Vicki smiled. "What are you doing here?"

Zeke put a hand on Chad's shoulder. "Take all the time you need. Vicki will show you to my office."

Vicki introduced Chad to the others, and baby Ryan crawled up to him and held out his hands. Chad grinned and picked the boy up. "I remember when you were just a little bump in your mother's tummy."

Finally, Vicki took Chad into the computer room to talk. "The girl who helped us get to your house—"

"Kelly Bradshaw?"

"Yeah, how is she?"

Chad shook his head. "The GC just about cleaned out all of us. They went house to house, looking for anyone without the mark. The ones they didn't find were ratted out by neighbors who'd seen us scrambling around in the night, trying to get food and supplies to each other. Kelly was caught about a month ago trying to get some water and bread to a woman on the other side of town." Chad looked away and wiped at his eyes.

"I'm so sorry. How did you survive?"

"Remember the woods behind my house where we went that night?"

Vicki nodded. Chad had been kind enough to make a picnic and share it with her one night. Their talk had helped her.

"A few of us escaped with all the food we could carry and started living there," Chad said. "We didn't think the GC would bother us, but some teenagers started exploring. You know what they'd do if they ever found us. I heard about Zeke and thought he might be able to give us some uniforms and chase them away."

"But how did you get here?" Vicki said. "A friend of mine has been trying for months to join us from Ohio, but they say it's too dangerous."

"Probably wasn't the smartest thing I've ever done. Took me a couple of nights and a few brushes with the GC, but I made it."

"But there had to be something more than just . . ." Vicki stopped. She remembered that Chad had expressed some feelings for her during their final moments in Iowa.

"The truth is, I really wanted to see you again," Chad said. "I don't know if you've thought of me at all since you were in Iowa, but I haven't stopped thinking about you. I've written a hundred e-mails, then trashed them."

Chad scooted his chair closer and leaned forward. "I see a strength in you and a love for others I'm drawn to. I know we weren't together that long and I don't know you that well, but I'd like to get to know you better."

Vicki blushed. "I don't know what to say."

"If you don't feel anything for me, I'll understand. I'll get back in my car, and you'll never hear from me again—"

Vicki put a hand on his arm. "I'm flattered, really. You were so kind to me when I was struggling."

"But there's someone else. The one in Ohio?"

"Yeah."

"He's a lucky guy. I appreciate you being honest with me." Chad stood and walked to the door.

"You didn't really come for Zeke's help?"

Chad turned. "All my friends are gone, Vicki. I'm the only one left."

Vicki stood. "Stay with us. You'll be safe."

Chad nodded and walked through the door. He was the last person Zeke helped with a Global Community uniform. The next night, Chad left without telling Vicki where he was going or what he was going to do.

Two days later a report came over GCNN of the arrest of a man posing as a Peacekeeper.

"The unidentified and unmarked man was apprehended in southeastern Indiana after a high-speed chase," the news anchor said over grainy video shot at night.

Shelly pointed at the screen. "That's Chad!"

"It is not known what type of terrorist plans the man had," the anchor continued, "but he was quickly processed and taken to the nearest loyalty enforcement facility."

Vicki looked at Zeke. "Did he tell you what he was going to do?"

Zeke took a breath. "He made me promise not to tell, but I guess it's okay now. He wanted to know where Judd was staying."

"Judd?"

"Chad said he was going to get him and bring him back here if it was the last thing he ever did."

Vicki put her face in her hands. "He was doing that for me."

"I tried to talk him into staying and waiting for things to cool down a bit, but he wouldn't listen."

The GC report continued, showing others who had been apprehended. Vicki wrote Judd and told him the bad news. They both promised each other they would wait until they were sure God wanted Judd to make the dangerous trip.

FIFTEEN

Heat Wave

THE COLD season had ended, and spring had come for Judd and the others hidden in Ohio. Judd flipped through a computer calendar and noticed the anniversary of the disappearances was only a day away. Even though it had been five years since his family had vanished, Judd felt the same ache as the first moment he walked into his house and realized they were gone and never coming back.

Five years of terror and beheadings and natural disasters. Five years of uncertainty, not knowing what was coming next.

Judd got out his notebook and looked at the things he had prayed about in the past few months. At the top of the list was:

Get to Wisconsin. That prayer hadn't been answered, but Judd hoped it would be soon.

Shelly and Conrad. There had been some misunderstanding in Wisconsin, and the two had gone from being best friends to enemies. Judd continued to ask God to give them a spirit of peace in the midst of turmoil.

Carpathia's failure. Though Judd knew those who had taken Carpathia's mark were doomed, he continued to pray for the failure of the Global Community and that the few undecided would turn to the true God. With hundreds of thousands dying because of the lack of drinkable water, that prayer was being answered every day. It seemed even those who followed Nicolae now realized they had been fooled by a cruel dictator who cared about no one but himself. As much as Carpathia, Leon Fortunato, and other GC authorities said it, the world wasn't getting better. Machines, computers, and people were wearing down. Services such as trash pickup and street cleaning were cut off. Roads fell into disrepair, and cities filled with crime.

Chang Wong. Judd continued to pray for his friend. He didn't know how Chang could stay in New Babylon, but he was still there, feeding information to the Tribulation Force and doing everything he could from the palace. Chang reported that the place had become a ghost town. Citizens no longer came to admire the sparkling buildings because the world was a mess. Half the population alive at the time of the Rapture had now died. Carpathia often called for the execution of leaders around the world who he thought weren't loyal enough, and Judd prayed that Chang would remain safe.

The undecided. Judd kept praying for new people to be reached by God's supernatural means. Every day he heard stories of angels preaching the Good News and the 144,000 Jewish evangelists spreading throughout the globe, preaching and teaching, apparently protected by angels. But Satan's evil forces were still at work. The deceivers were going strong, trying to convince everyone that they did their miracles by Nicolae's power. Judd wept at scenes of unmarked people in a remote Philippine village being lured with the promise of water. Though the Global Community News Network didn't show it, Judd knew the same thing that happened near Petra had probably happened to these unfortunate people.

Tsion Ben-Judah. Judd prayed for strength for the leader of a growing mass of people dedicated to following God no matter what the cost. Tsion continually taught that God was evening the score with the evil ruler. *It is not as if the God of gods could not defeat any foe he chooses,* Dr. Ben-Judah wrote, *but the stench of the other side evangelizing for evil has offended him and kindled his wrath. Yet the wrath of God remains balanced by his great mercy and love. There has been not one report of death or injury to any of the 144,000 evangelists God has raised up to spread the truth about his Son.*

Rayford Steele. The leader of the Tribulation Force wrote Judd that he had also felt the presence of angels protecting him and his flyers as they moved about the world. God had protected these freedom flyers from harm in the Middle East, and he had done so over other areas as well when the GC tried to intercept them and force them to land. Judd asked God to continue guarding these brave pilots.

Buck and Chloe Williams. Judd prayed for Buck's writing in *The Truth,* which was still read by millions throughout the world. Chloe had massive duties with the Co-op, as well as being a mother to little Kenny.

Jacques Madeleine. Judd never forgot the kindness of his friends in France. Though the GC had discovered the anti-Carpathia action at the man's chalet, the group had been able to hide until the GC moved on. From the last report, many had become believers through the ministry.

Westin Jakes. Z-Van's former pilot had been

put to work for the Tribulation Force and flew missions around the world. Westin had written many e-mails detailing the harrowing experiences over major cities, but each time God had delivered them from certain death.

Lionel. The transition for Lionel had been difficult. He felt the "phantom pain" of his missing arm, and many days he couldn't sleep because of his experience under the rock. Lionel had been tight-lipped about this, not even sharing with Judd about that night. Judd didn't press him for information but continued to pray with him and find things for Lionel to do.

There were other names on Judd's list like Mac McCullum, Leah Rose, Hannah Palemoon, and Naomi Tiberius, people Judd knew from the Tribulation Force and his travels to Petra. Judd thought often of Nada's parents and asked God to comfort them with the loss of their son and daughter. Judd prayed for Mark, Conrad, and the others in Wisconsin regularly, especially when Vicki brought up a situation. He remembered all the people who had given Lionel and him shelter while traveling north, and he asked God to protect them until the Glorious Appearing.

Finally, Judd prayed for Vicki. He asked

God to draw her close and make her an even stronger believer than she already was. Judd thanked God for Vicki's friendship, her support, and for the life she had brought to him, even separated by the miles. "If I didn't have friends like Vicki and Lionel and Mark . . . I don't know if I'd have the will to keep on going."

One evening after a meeting with their Ohio group, Judd opened an e-mail from Sam Goldberg alerting Judd to the fact that the seas of the world had turned from blood to salt water again.

Tsion said this morning that he has been given no special knowledge about this by God, but he wonders if something worse is coming soon.

Judd turned on GCNN and found Carpathia taking credit for lifting the plague. "My people created a formula that has healed the waters." Nicolae beamed. "The plant and animal life of the oceans will surge back to life before long. And now that the oceans are clear again, all our beautiful lake and river waterways will soon be restored as well."

As usual, Carpathia was wrong. The plague of blood lifted from the seas, but as a few more weeks went by it was clear that God had chosen to let the lakes and rivers remain blood-filled. Judd wondered if Tsion was right. Was something worse headed for the earth? Judd opened his Bible to the book of Revelation and studied the text and Tsion's writings side by side.

🌟

Vicki looked for any ray of hope for Judd and Lionel to come north over the next few months but found none. There hadn't been another visitor for Zeke since Chad Harris, so the only movement about the country by believers was done by the commodity Co-op, and even that was kept to a minimum. Reports of drivers being stopped, pulled onto the street, and immediately shot were common.

The United North American States had become one of the unhealthiest places on earth to live, and Vicki wished she had taken Judd up on his offer to move to France. Or, she thought, they could have hidden out in Petra. There they were sure to have food, water, and safety.

But Vicki tried not to think of what could have been. Dealing with reality was a full-time job. Baby Ryan had become toddler Ryan, and while the boy's laughter and play habits brought joy to everyone in the camp (especially Charlie and Zeke who made him wooden blocks and toys), more tension had arisen between the Fogartys and Ryan's mother. Cheryl had become moody, staying in her cabin for days at a time and lashing out at anyone who tried to help her.

Vicki grew frustrated, running out of ideas. Josey and Tom Fogarty became fearful that Cheryl might do something careless with the boy when she had him in her cabin. While Ryan was with her, she seemed to become more cheery, but when he returned to the Fogartys, a cloud came over her.

Vicki prayed nonstop for Cheryl, but the Fogartys called a meeting with Vicki and a few others and asked that Cheryl not be able to see the boy alone. "We're too scared she might take off with him," Josey said. "We love Cheryl, and she's given us the greatest gift we could ever receive, but she's just not stable."

"I've noticed the same thing," Mark said. "She's telling Ryan mean things about Josey and Tom."

"What's she saying?" Vicki said.

Mark sighed. "I was walking by her cabin while she was out at the swing Charlie rigged between the trees. She told Ryan over and over that she was his real mother, that the Fogartys were only taking care of him, and that she was going to take him away as soon as she found a place to go."

Vicki shook her head. "I agree that's terrible, but if you don't let her see him anymore, she could get worse."

"We're going to have to take that chance," Tom said.

Cheryl flew into a rage when Vicki tried to talk with her about the situation. Marshall, Tom, and Zeke came inside when the girl began throwing things. They tried praying with her, but finally Marshall gave her something to make her sleep.

The next few weeks were some of the most difficult Vicki had ever lived through. There were shrieks and cries at night, and Cheryl would show up at the Fogartys' door, asking to see Ryan. It reminded her of the time at the schoolhouse when the locusts had stung Janie and Melinda.

Finally, Marshall and the others decided they would either have to find a new place for Cheryl or move the Fogartys and Ryan. Everyone felt sad for Cheryl but agreed something had to be done.

Vicki tried one last time to talk with her and explain the situation. Cheryl had been so sweet and had learned so much about the Bible, but now she didn't show up at their regular meetings and seemed hostile when they talked about Scripture.

Cheryl sat in a dark corner of the room,

her hair hanging in front of her face while Vicki spoke. "Is there something going on you want to talk about?"

"Yeah, they've taken my baby away."

"But you wanted the Fogartys to have Ryan. Remember?"

Cheryl ran a hand through her hair. "I've changed my mind."

Vicki scooted closer and put a hand on the girl's arm. Cheryl recoiled and pulled both feet into her chair.

"Cheryl, we're really concerned about you. The way you're acting . . . this is not you. I know the kind and gentle person you are, and what you've become lately is somebody different. Please talk to me."

Cheryl set her jaw and didn't look at Vicki. "Get out. And don't come back until you bring my baby."

Vicki wept as she left. Marshall and the others looked for a safe place for Cheryl.

✺

Sam rushed to the communications center when he heard news about something strange in Petra. He found Naomi Tiberius with Abdullah Smith and several of the leaders, including Dr. Tsion Ben-Judah and Chaim Rosenzweig.

Sam had heard from Chang Wong in New Babylon that something was up with Carpathia. Chang had overheard a conversation between Nicolae and his staff lamenting the fact that people in Petra had clean water to drink while the rest of the world suffered. Chang was worried that the GC might try something drastic to tap into the same spring that nourished Petra.

Sam stood in the back of the communications center, close enough to hear the conversation. A missile was fifteen minutes away, and by Abdullah's calculations was headed for a spot where the Global Community had been drilling for water.

Sam went outside to an area overlooking the desert. Sure enough, the GC workers had pulled back. Sam wiped his forehead and looked at the sun. Was it just him or had it gotten hotter? It was almost ten in the morning, but the heat felt like the hottest part of the afternoon.

The leaders and Abdullah walked onto a ledge and looked at the work site. A few minutes later a bright speck moved toward Petra. The missile struck the desert and raised a huge cloud of sand and soil. The explosion roared like thunder, and the ground shook. But no water or blood geyser spouted from the missile that must have cost millions of Nicks. Sam shook his head at the foolishness of the Global Community and wiped his brow again.

🌵

Chang's first inkling that something was wrong came as he secretly listened to a conversation coming from Carpathia's office. He had become more and more bold with his listening habits, wearing headphones at his desk so he could follow news of the missile.

Carpathia was upset that their weapon hadn't produced anything more than a crater.

A knock on the door and Krystall, Nicolae's secretary, entered. "Begging your pardon, sir, but we are getting strange reports."

"What kind of reports?"

"Some kind of a heat wave. The lines are jammed. People are—"

Suddenly, shouts came from Chang's office mates. He closed his computer program and took off the headphones. He noticed Rasha by the window with another man named Lars. They were pointing to the street, obviously upset.

Chang heard an explosion, then another, as people crowded around him.

"Get back!" Chang's boss, Aurelio Figueroa, shouted as he burst into the room waving his arms. "Get away from the windows!"

It was too late for Rasha and Lars. The window in front of them gave way, sending shards of glass flying about the room. Both were struck by the broken glass and crumpled to the floor as others screamed. Hot, steamy air blew into the room. A woman tried to help her fallen friends, but her hair curled, then burst into flames from the heat.

"What *is* this?" someone shrieked. "What's happening?"

Chang had the same question. Was this something Nicolae had planned, or was it God's work? And would believers be affected like those with Carpathia's mark?

Judd awoke to a phone call from an excited Chang Wong. Judd felt groggy and missed the first few words from his friend. Something about heat and people dying.

"Slow down," Judd said, wiping his eyes. "What's going on?"

"The fourth Bowl Judgment from God," Chang said. "I'll explain in a moment, but you must be prepared."

"You mean we're in danger?" Judd said, suddenly awake.

"I don't think so. I think believers will be spared, while this will be a nightmare for unbelievers. But this may be our chance to move much-needed supplies to you and your friends."

Judd's heart raced. He was excited about the prospect of food and supplies for the Ohio group. But the thing that excited him most was that if they could move supplies more easily, *he* might be able to move, and that meant he might get to Wisconsin. *Back to Vicki.*

ABOUT THE AUTHORS

Jerry B. Jenkins (www.jerryjenkins.com) is the writer of the Left Behind series. He owns the Jerry B. Jenkins Christian Writers Guild, an organization dedicated to mentoring aspiring authors. Former vice president for publishing for the Moody Bible Institute of Chicago, he also served many years as editor of *Moody* magazine and is now Moody's writer-at-large.

His writing has appeared in publications as varied as *Reader's Digest, Parade, Guideposts,* in-flight magazines, and dozens of other periodicals. Jenkins's biographies include books with Billy Graham, Hank Aaron, Bill Gaither, Luis Palau, Walter Payton, Orel Hershiser, and Nolan Ryan, among many others. His books appear regularly on the *New York Times, USA Today, Wall Street Journal,* and *Publishers Weekly* bestseller lists.

Jerry is also the writer of the nationally syndicated sports story comic strip *Gil Thorp,* distributed to newspapers across the United States by Tribune Media Services.

Jerry and his wife, Dianna, live in Colorado and have three grown sons.

Dr. Tim LaHaye (www.timlahaye.com), who conceived the idea of fictionalizing an account of the Rapture and the Tribulation, is a noted author, minister, and nationally recognized speaker on Bible prophecy. He is the founder of both Tim LaHaye Ministries and The PreTrib Research Center. He also recently cofounded the Tim LaHaye School of Prophecy at Liberty University. Presently Dr. LaHaye speaks at many of the major Bible prophecy conferences in the U.S. and Canada, where his current prophecy books are very popular.

Dr. LaHaye holds a doctor of ministry degree from Western Theological Seminary and a doctor of literature degree from Liberty University. For twenty-five years he pastored one of the nation's outstanding churches in San Diego, which grew to three locations. It was during that time that he founded two accredited Christian high schools, a Christian school system of ten schools, and Christian Heritage College.

Dr. LaHaye has written over forty books that have been published in more than thirty languages. He has written books on a wide variety of subjects, such as family life, temperaments, and Bible prophecy. His current fiction works, the Left Behind series, written with Jerry B. Jenkins, continue to appear on the bestseller lists of the Christian Booksellers Association, *Publishers Weekly*, *Wall Street Journal*, *USA Today*, and the *New York Times*.

He is the father of four grown children and grandfather of nine. Snow skiing, waterskiing, motorcycling, golfing, vacationing with family, and jogging are among his leisure activities.

The Future Is Clear

Check out the exciting Left Behind: The Kids series

BOOKS #37 AND #38 COMING SOON!

Discover the latest about the Left Behind series and complete line of products at

www.leftbehind.com